"You don't expect *me* to go look for him!"

Cody's words triggered Shannon's anger. "I wouldn't ask you to do it for nothing," she snapped. "I'll pay to charter your plane."

"It isn't the money." He ground out the words. "I don't want it."

"Then what is it?" Shannon demanded impatiently.

A low groan escaped his throat. "Surely you've guessed by now, Texas." He pulled her roughly to him, bringing her within inches of his mouth. "Why should I help you find Rick when I want you for myself?"

No reply was permitted as he hungrily took possession of her lips. "I can make you forget him...." His husky voice vibrated against the sensitive skin of her neck.

And in a cold breath of sanity Shannon discovered that he could.

JANET DAILEY AMERICANA

NORTHERN MAGIC

Harlequin Books

TORONTO • NEW YORK • LONDON
AMSTERDAM • PARIS • SYDNEY • HAMBURG
STOCKHOLM • ATHENS • TOKYO • MILAN
MADRID • WARSAW • BUDAPEST • AUCKLAND

The state flower depicted on the cover of this book is forget-me-not.

Janet Dailey Americana edition published June 1986
Second printing March 1988
Third printing April 1989
Fourth printing April 1990
Fifth printing April 1991
Sixth printing May 1991
Seventh printing March 1992

ISBN 0-373-21902-4

Harlequin Presents edition published January 1982

Original hardcover edition published in 1982
by Mills & Boon Limited

NORTHERN MAGIC

Dedication

To my Bill, who has always encouraged, organized and managed me. He is reluctant to take credit for his efforts on my behalf— whether in the research and editing or the business and management side of my career.

This liberated lady doesn't mind admitting that I wouldn't have achieved all that I have to this date if it weren't for my husband.

This is for you, Bill, with all my love.

CHAPTER ONE

As THE plane broke through the clouds blanketing Anchorage in a gray shroud, Shannon Hayes strained to catch a glimpse of Alaska's largest city through the plane's scratched window. A dark murky wall of mountains loomed close to the city, their peaks lost in the cloud cover. Below there was a scattering of homes and an interweaving of roads. In the distance a few tall buildings rose to identify the city center, their rectangular gray shapes disappearing into the sky's low ceiling.

Brief surprise registered at the smallness of the city; she had been expecting a bustling metropolis, perhaps a scaled-down version of Houston, Texas, her own hometown. The thought didn't last long—it was almost instantly overpowered by the excitement of seeing her destination at last.

Shannon's brown eyes were shining as she leaned back in her seat. A smile hovered at the corners of her mouth in anticipation of the joy she would find at journey's end. She touched the engagement ring on her left hand, rubbing the surface of the square-cut diamond as if it were a talisman. The gray gloom outside the aircraft's window could not dampen her eagerness.

There was the thud of the wheels on the airport runway, followed within seconds by the reversing thrust of the jet engines to slow the craft down. It had the opposite effect on her pulse, which picked up tempo to beat faster. She ran exploring fingers over the dark chestnut length of her hair, seeking any strand that might have strayed out of place and finding none. Not twenty minutes before she had brushed fullness into its windblown style and freshened her makeup. Shannon wanted to look her best when Rick met his "dark-haired, dark-eyed beauty"—his descriptive phrase for her.

It had been long and lonely months since she'd seen Rick. She could remember the tears she'd shed at the airport the day he left for Alaska, the promises they'd made to each other and the desperate quality that had marked their kisses. The letters and the phone calls from Rick had been few and far between, incapable of filling the emptiness that came with their separation.

Rick had promised that the minute he had a secure job and a place for them to live he'd send for her. Neither had anticipated it would take so long. The last letter Shannon had received from him had come more than a month ago, the end of July. She'd heard nothing more from him until the envelope arrived on the first of

September. It had contained a one-way ticket to Anchorage and nothing more—no letter, no note—but the message was loud and clear: Rick wanted her with him. The niggling fear that he might have stopped loving her was banished, and Shannon was on her way to his arms.

It had taken her a week to make the arrangements to move and pack all her belongings—some to take with her and the rest to be shipped. Her parents would be flying in on the coming weekend for the wedding. They were convinced she and Rick were both crazy for leaving the warm Gulf Coast of Texas to make a home in the frigid climate of Alaska. But Shannon understood Rick's thirst for adventure and his desire to participate in the development of America's last frontier. To a certain extent she shared his feelings, but she was realistic enough to know it wouldn't be paradise.

Although her parents had done everything they could to discourage the move, they wisely didn't object. At twenty-three, Shannon hardly needed their consent to marry. She had been engaged to Rick for more than a year now, so marriage wasn't something she was rushing into blindly.

She was only seconds away from being reunited with her fiancé as the plane taxied to the terminal building. When the seat-belt sign flashed off, Shannon gathered her overnight case from beneath the seat in front of her and collected the blue wool parka from the overhead bin, then joined the queue of disembarking passengers.

Despite the burden of her shoulder bag, the overnight case and the heavy coat, her steps were light and quick as she left the plane via the airliner tunnel. She scanned the small crowd waiting in the gate area, looking for Rick's tall lanky frame and that familiar shock of sandy blond hair. She was oblivious to the interested and admiring glances she received as she skipped over the faces of strangers in search of Rick.

When she didn't immediately see him, her steps slowed. She was accidentally jostled from behind by a fellow passenger and moved out of the mainstream to look around the gate area again for Rick. The brown radiance that had lighted her eyes now held a glitter of confusion. He was nowhere in sight.

Shannon lingered in the corridor outside the arrival gate until all the passengers were off the plane and had either been met or continued to the baggage-claim section of the terminal. But Rick never came.

She had sent a telegram advising him of her arrival time. What could have gone wrong? She moved to follow the other passengers to the baggage area and claim her luggage. The thought occurred to her that Rick might be waiting for her there, and her steps quickened.

But he wasn't there, either. Or parked outside in the loading zone. Surrounded by the three-piece luggage set, Shannon stood beneath the terminal overhang and stared through the drizzle at the grayness cast over everything by the clouds.

Trying not to worry over his failure to meet her, she found excuses to explain why he wasn't there. Maybe he was working and unable to take time off to meet her; but he could have left a message for her. That left only two alternatives: either there had been an error in the telegram she'd sent, listing the wrong time of arrival, or he hadn't received it. But Rick *was* expecting her. He had sent for her.

With a determined thrust to her chin, Shannon decided on a plan of action. There was obviously a mix-up somewhere, so there was no point in waiting at the airport any longer. She motioned to a waiting taxicab. The driver stepped out, running an appreciative glance over her while maintaining a respectful attitude. He wasn't much older than Shannon, dressed in a pale blue Windbreaker, its collar turned up against the drizzle.

"Sorry." He smiled at her. "I saw you standing there, but I thought you were waiting for someone."

"I was, but. . . he was obviously detained and couldn't come to pick me up." She voiced the excuse she had been making over and over in her head.

"Something probably came up at the last minute," the young cabdriver suggested.

Hearing someone else say the same thing she had been thinking reassured her that it was probably the truth. While he began loading her luggage into the trunk, Shannon slid into the rear seat of the taxi and opened her shoulder purse to look for Rick's last letter with his Anchorage address.

The driver climbed behind the wheel and half turned to glance at her. "Where to, miss?"

"Northern Lights Boulevard," Shannon replied, certain of the street. Then she found the letter and gave him the address of Rick's apartment, their future home together.

As they drove away from the terminal building and the row of commercial hangars, the young man glanced into the rearview mirror at Shannon's reflection. "Is this your first trip to Alaska?"

"Yes." Her gaze strayed out the window, her concern for Rick's absence lessening to the point where she could take in her new surroundings. "It's much greener than I expected." She observed the house lawns and the grassy verges of the road. The blue wool parka was heavy on her lap. The cable-knit pullover sweater she was wearing over her lavender silk blouse provided more than enough warmth. "And warmer than I expected it to be in September."

"You had visions of an ice-encrusted city, didn't you?" the driver chuckled softly.

"Well—" her laugh was low and slightly self-condemning "—I don't think I'm going to need

the long underwear in my suitcase for a while."
Her smile deepened at the sight of flowers
blooming in house gardens.

"The climate here isn't as inhospitable as
some people on the outside think. As a matter of
fact, Anchorage weather can be quite agreeable,
although it is colder in the interior around Fairbanks," he admitted.

"Are you from here?" she wondered aloud,
since he spoke so knowledgeably.

"I'm a native Alaskan. I was born here."
There was pride in the admission, a pride that
was quickly tempered with humor. "Three years
ago I went down to the lower forty-eight to visit
some relatives in California, but I came back—
which shows you how stupid I am."

Shannon laughed, as she was supposed to do.
His friendliness was natural, not due solely to
her being an attractive woman. "I doubt that."

"It's late in the season for tourists. Are you
visiting? Or are you planning to move here?"

"Yes, I'll be settling here." It was a decisive
answer.

"Do you have people here? Friends?" the
driver asked curiously.

"My fiancé," Shannon replied, and glimpsed
the disappointment that flickered across the
man's reflection in the rearview mirror.

"I see," he murmured as he turned off the
thoroughfare onto a main cross street. "What
does he do?"

"He's a pilot," she explained.

"Who isn't around here?" The young man laughed shortly. "Sometimes I think there are more planes than cars. Flying is the only way to reach some of the remote regions of Alaska. Does he work for one of the major airlines?"

"No." Once that had been Rick's ambition—until he'd heard stories about the Alaskan bush pilots. After that he considered flying commercial airliners to be a tamely routine operation. "He has a job with a private charter service."

"That's good. Year-round jobs aren't that easy to come by in Alaska, regardless of the propaganda you hear."

He slowed the taxi and stopped in front of a nondescript two-story building painted beige. "This is it." He gestured toward the apartment block to indicate they had reached her destination. When Shannon paid him the fare, he pocketed it and said, "I'll carry your luggage inside for you."

Leaving the cab, she walked to the central entrance and opened the door. Rick's apartment number was on the door opposite the one marked Manager. Although she didn't expect Rick to be home, she knocked on his door anyway on the off chance he could be. There was no immediate answer. Hoping the manager would let her into the apartment to wait for Rick, Shannon turned away just as the door opened a crack.

She swung swiftly around to face the door again, a smile of happy surprise lighting her expression—only to be wiped away by the sight of the whiskered man peering out the door. A rough-looking character in his late forties, he gave her a bleary-eyed stare, raking her up and down.

"Whatever you're selling, lady, I'm not buying," he declared gruffly, and shut the door.

The cabdriver entered with her luggage as Shannon recovered from her shock at seeing a total stranger in Rick's apartment. There was probably a logical explanation for his presence. Maybe Rick was sharing the apartment to keep down the cost.

She knocked again. This time the door was jerked open and the stoop-shouldered man blocked the way.

"Look, lady," he said with ill-patience, "I work nights. I don't like being woke up in the middle of the afternoon, so why don't you knock on somebody else's door."

"I'm looking for Rick Farris," she rushed, because she had the feeling he was going to slam the door on her again.

"Never heard of him." The door started to close.

"But this is his apartment," Shannon protested with a frown.

"Lady, I don't know what your game is." He eyed her with exasperation. "But this is *my* apartment. The name is Jack Morrow, and there is nobody living here but me."

"There must be some mistake." Her frown

deepened as she began rummaging through her purse for Rick's letter.

"If there is a mistake, you are the one who made it," he retorted unkindly, then softened sufficiently to suggest, "Check with the manager. Maybe the guy you're looking for lives in one of the other apartments. Ask him and let me get some sleep."

The door had already closed by the time Shannon had found the letter in her shoulder bag. She double-checked the envelope, but she was certain the address of the apartment was the same. Confused, she turned and found herself facing the young cabdriver with her luggage at his feet. He was wearing a sympathetic expression.

"Check with the manager," he advised. "Your boyfriend could have changed apartments or found a cheaper place to live."

"I suppose." Shannon conceded the possibility, but surely Rick would have let her know?

"I'll wait for you...just in case," the cabby volunteered.

"Thank you," she murmured, and crossed the entryway to the manager's door, keeping Rick's letter in hand. She knocked twice and heard shuffling steps approach in answer to her summons.

An older man of retirement age opened the door and peered at her over the top of half-lensed glasses. He spied her suitcases sitting in the hall and darted a sharp look at her.

"My name is Shannon Hayes—" she began.

"I'm sorry, miss," he interrupted, making his own guess as to why she was there. "We don't have any vacancies right now. I'll be glad to put your name on the waiting list, but there's already four ahead of you."

"No, you don't understand. I'm looking for Rick Farris. I'm his fiancé." Shannon attempted again to explain.

"So he ran out on you, too," the apartment manager harrumphed. "If you find him, tell him he owes me a week's rent. When he pays it I'll give him back the stuff he left."

"Rick isn't here?" An icy chill of uneasiness ran up her spine.

"I thought that was what I just said." The older gentleman cocked his head to one side.

"Didn't he leave a forwarding address?" The sensation of alarm was beginning to grow. None of this sounded like Rick. He plotted things through very thoroughly, then went ahead—just like piloting an aircraft. First he laid out a course, then he flew it. He'd sent her an airplane ticket but hadn't been at the airport to meet her when she arrived. Now she learned that he had moved out of the apartment.

"No, he didn't leave a forwarding address," the manager replied. "He didn't even give me notice he was leaving. I wouldn't have suspected he was going except two weeks ago, just a couple of days before the rent was due, I saw him coming out of his apartment with a suitcase. I reminded him the rent was coming due. 'Course he told me that he'd be back in time to take care of it, but I never saw hide nor hair of him after that."

The manager shook his head, indicating by the gesture that it was an old story. "I must admit he fooled me. He seemed a real likable fellow. I waited a week before I rented the apartment to someone else."

"Do you mean Rick hasn't been here for two weeks?" Shannon asked, realization dawning. "Then he couldn't have received the telegram I sent him, telling him when I would arrive."

"Telegram? A telegram did come for him a few days ago." The old man straightened slightly and tipped his head down to peer at Shannon again over the rim of his half glasses. "I didn't know where to send it on to, so I kept it here. Thought he might stop by for his things."

"What did Rick leave here?" she questioned. "May I see?"

The manager hesitated. "You can see, but I can't let you take anything," he agreed at last, and stepped out of the doorway to let her enter his apartment. "I packed it all in a couple of boxes. There isn't much of any value in it." He motioned toward the two boxes sitting in the corner of the living room. "If he doesn't come for them pretty soon, I'm going to have to store them in the upstairs attic to get them out of my way."

Shannon crouched down to unfold the flaps

of one box. Mostly it contained odds and ends and a few clothes—the everyday sort of worn shirts and jeans. In the second box she found a gold-framed photograph of herself, the one she had signed to him, "With all my love." Her fingers tightened on it.

"Rick wouldn't have left this behind," she murmured to herself. There was nothing wrong with the manager's hearing. A look of pity was on his face when she looked up. "That day you saw him with the suitcase, did Rick say where he was going?"

"Nope." He shook his head. "And I didn't ask. At the time I didn't think it was any of my business."

"This isn't like Rick." Again, Shannon said it mostly to herself.

"People change," he shrugged.

"No." She wouldn't accept that argument as she laid the photograph back in the box and stood upright. "There is a reason for this. I don't know what it is, but I'm going to find out...somehow."

"Good luck to you," was the skeptical encouragement from the manager.

"Thank you." Shannon opened the flap of her shoulder purse and reached inside for her leather wallet. "How much does Rick owe you? I'll pay for it and take his things with me."

The manager drew back. "I don't want to be taking your money, miss."

"It's all right," she assured him. "Rick and I are going to be married."

He hesitated, then grudgingly named an amount as if it went against his character to take money from a woman for a man's debt. While he wrote out a receipt at a small desk for the money she'd paid him, Shannon picked up one of the boxes and carried it into the building's foyer, where the young cabdriver waited near her luggage.

"Did you find out anything?" the driver asked quietly.

She shook her head, chestnut hair brushing her shoulders. "There is another box inside. Would you mind carrying it out?"

"Be happy to," he assured her, and entered the manager's apartment as the old man walked out to give Shannon her receipt.

"If you should hear from Rick, or if he stops by, would you tell him that I'm staying at...." She stopped and glanced beyond the man to the cabdriver, returning with the box in his arms. She had anticipated that Rick would make arrangements for a hotel. She addressed her question to the driver. "What is the name of a good hotel in Anchorage, a well-known place that's centrally located?"

"The Westward?" He named one, then quickly named two more to give her a choice. "Or there's Captain Cook's and the Sheffield House."

"I'll be staying at the Westward." Shannon chose the first.

"I'll tell him," the manager promised, but his attitude showed that he doubted he would have the opportunity to pass the message along.

When she left the building to carry the box to the taxi, the cloud cover seemed to be hanging lower, darkening everything. A fine mist was falling, replacing the earlier drizzle. The damp chill in the air seemed to penetrate to her bones. So many unexplained things had happened, her anxiety increased from the weight of them. One question kept repeating itself: where was Rick?

The cabdriver took the box from her and stowed it in the trunk, then helped her into the rear seat. "You wait here while I get the rest of your luggage," he instructed.

Sitting alone in the silence of the cab, Shannon tried very hard not to think the worst. Just because Rick wasn't at the apartment didn't necessarily mean that he had been injured or become ill. There were probably several explanations—even if she couldn't think of a single one. She didn't know where he was, but that didn't mean he was missing. Yet nothing made sense. She was confused and worried.

"Do you want me to take you to the Westward?" The driver slipped behind the wheel and closed the door.

"Yes, please."

He turned in his seat and noticed how tightly her hands were clasped together in her lap.

"There probably isn't anything to be upset about. When you finally see him, you'll more than likely laugh about this wild-goose chase around Anchorage."

"Probably," Shannon agreed, and managed a brief smile at the gentle reassurance.

Facing the front again, he started the motor, then paused before shifting it into gear. "It's possible that he might be trying to reach you. He didn't get your telegram, so he doesn't know you're here," he reminded her. "Is there someone you can call in Texas to see if he has been trying to contact you?"

"Yes." She'd call her parents the instant she reached the hotel. Then she realized she hadn't told the cabdriver where she was from. "How did you know I'm from Texas?"

A wide grin split his face. "It's kinda hard to mistake that soft drawl," he explained. "It isn't the heavy twang of some Texans I've met, but it's there just the same."

The corners of her mouth relaxed into a natural smile. "I should have guessed." It was difficult to remember that most people thought *she* had an accent.

Her smile faded as the cab pulled onto the street. His comment served to remind her that she was in unfamiliar territory. The city was strange to her. She knew no one except Rick, and she didn't know where he was.

The traffic became heavier near the center of the city, demanding more of the driver's attention. He pointed out some of the landmarks. Shannon looked, but she was too preoccupied with her own concerns to have much interest in the sights around her.

At the hotel entrance there was a porter to take her luggage into the lobby. After she'd paid the driver, he gave her a card with his phone number written on it. "My name is Andy," he told her. "If you need some help locating your boyfriend, give me a call."

"Thank you." She was touched by his offer. "As you said, it's probably all a silly misunderstanding."

Crossing the expansive lobby, she filled out the necessary registration forms and was shown to a room on the fifth floor. She went directly to the telephone and placed a call to her parents. It was her mother who answered.

"It's me—Shannon," she identified herself.

"I've been wondering about you. Are you in Alaska? Did you make it safely? I'll bet you're frozen solid." There was hardly a break between sentences as her mother rushed the words. "You should have taken warmer clothes with you. Do you want me to ship some of your things up to you by air, rather than wait until your father and I come this weekend?"

"No. The weather is fine, mom," Shannon assured her, then felt that statement needed some qualification. "It's no different from Houston in the winter—gray, drizzling and cool."

"Are you sure?" her mother questioned skeptically. "Velma Jo and Fred were there two years ago and said they practically froze to death."

"I promise you I'm not freezing." She took a breath to ask if Rick had called, and her mother took advantage of the scant second of silence.

"How was the plane trip? What is there—four hours' time difference? I never can figure those things out. I'll bet you're suffering from jet lag, aren't you, Shannon? Traveling is so tiring on its own without someone messing with the clock."

"Yes, I...." She supposed she was tired. She'd been too worried about Rick to notice.

Her mother's voice became muffled. "I'm talking to Shannon. She's calling from Alaska," she was saying to someone else in the room.

"Who is that, mom?" Shannon was struck by the laughable thought that it might be Rick. How ironic if he had flown to Texas to accompany her personally on the long flight!

"It's your father. He wants to say hello." The telephone was obviously passed to her father, because Shannon heard his voice speaking to her a second later. "Hi, honey, how are you?"

"I'm fine, dad."

"How is my future son-in-law? I suppose he's there with you."

Which meant he wasn't there. With a sinking

heart she realized that it also meant Rick hadn't called her parents' home. There was no message for her.

"Actually...he isn't here," she admitted, trying not to let her concern creep into her voice.

"Oh?" It was a pregnant sound. "Didn't he meet you at the airport?"

"No. It seems he didn't receive my telegram," Shannon explained, at least partially. She considered confiding in her father, then realized he was too far away to help. Besides, she might be needlessly alarming her parents. "Rick is...out of town right now."

"How soon will he be back?" He had barely asked the question when his voice became muffled; obviously, he was explaining the situation to her mother.

"I'm not sure," she answered. "I haven't talked to Rick yet." Which was the truth.

"His employer knows when he'll come back, doesn't he?" he asked.

A ray of hope glistened. "I'm going to call and find out." Why hadn't she thought of contacting Rick's employer before? He would know Rick's whereabouts, his new address, everything. "I just wanted to let you and mom know I had arrived safely."

CHAPTER TWO

ANOTHER FIVE MINUTES went by before the conversation with her parents finally came to a close. Afterward Shannon ransacked her large purse again in search of the letter from Rick, which contained the name of his employer. She found it—Steele Air. Flipping open the telephone book, she ran her finger down the column of *S*'s and stopped when she found Steele Air. She picked up the receiver and dialed the number.

On the sixth ring a man answered, "Steele Air. No matter where you wanta go, we'll take you there." There was a rasping edge to the male voice that hinted at advanced age.

Shannon smiled at the slogan so proudly recited. "I would like to speak to Rick Farris, please."

There was a pause. "Who?"

"Rick Farris," she repeated, and added, "He's a pilot."

"Who ain't?" was the retort, but a reply wasn't expected. A hand was cupped over the mouthpiece of the receiver on the other end of the line, muffling the voice that spoke to someone else. A second later the same rasping voice returned to the line. "There's no one here by that name."

"Wait a minute," Shannon said quickly, in case the man intended to hang up. "Do you have a phone number where I could reach him?"

There was another lengthy pause. "We don't have his phone number."

"Can you tell me how I might contact him?" she persisted.

"Miss, I really don't know." The voice sounded indifferent and dryly amused.

"How do you get hold of him?" There had to be some way.

"Why would we want to?"

"He works for you," she replied, and began to wonder if she wasn't being given the runaround as a kind of joke.

"What?" The man sounded startled. "What did you say his name was?"

"Rick Farris."

"We don't have any pilots working for us by that name. You probably want one of the other charter outfits," came the patient yet gruff reply.

"No." Shannon glanced at Rick's letter again. It plainly read Steele Air. "This is Steele Air, isn't it?"

"Yes, but there's no Rick Farris here," he stated, very positively.

It finally sank in that he meant it. "Thank

you," she murmured, and heard the click of the phone being hung up. Slowly she replaced the receiver on the cradle.

Tiny lines creased her forehead as she picked up Rick's letter and began reading it through again word by word. It was filled with information Rick had gleaned about the owner/operator of the service—a man named Cody Steele. Nowhere did it say that Rick had been hired, yet the implication was strong.

Her frustration mounted. The letter was a month old, but it was the only clue she had. Someone with Steele Air had to know something about Rick. If not the man who'd answered the phone, then someone else.

Shannon started to reach for the telephone to call back, then changed her mind and scribbled down the address of Steele Air on the back of the letter's envelope. Grabbing her purse, she slipped the leather strap over her shoulder and dropped the room key inside.

Five minutes later she was in the hotel lobby downstairs, requesting a taxi. One responded immediately to the call. As she crawled inside and gave the driver the address at Marrill Field, Shannon was almost sorry she hadn't asked for the young driver named Andy, for moral support.

Instead of taking her to the Anchorage International Airport, where she had arrived by jet, the cab drove to another airfield closer to the heart of the city. Shannon couldn't recall ever

seeing so many small planes in one place in all
her life. They passed row after row of hangars,
with single- and twin-engine aircrafts parked
inside or tied down on the concrete aprons outside. There was a multitude of aviation companies, so many that the names began to run
together in her mind.

When the cab turned and stopped in front of
one of the hangars and its attached office, Shannon stared at the sign across the front that read
Steele Air. It was a full minute before realization sank in that she had reached her destination. Except for the sign, there was nothing to
distinguish this outfit from any of the other flying services.

With the fare paid, she stepped out of the cab
into the misting rain. After a second's hesitation
she walked toward the door of the concrete-
block building that adjoined the metal hangar.
Her boots made small splashes in the gathering
puddles of water, ripples ringing out from her
footsteps.

Entering the building, she paused inside the
door to wipe her high-heeled boots on the bristled mat—a consideration others hadn't observed, judging by the muddy tracks on the tiled
floor. Her entrance had brought a halt to the
conversation in the small office area.

The long room that ran the length of the
building was decidedly informal, more of a
waiting area than an actual office. Aeronautical
charts were tacked on the walls along with

photographs, plaques and a bulletin board
crowded with cards, advertisements and notes
scribbled on torn slips of paper. There was a
desk, its metal sides scratched and dented. The
swivel chair behind it was vacant and showed
signs of wear.

The coffee table was littered with aviation
magazines and overflowing ashtrays. One of the
men sitting on the green vinyl couch was using
the table for a footstool, his feet propped on top
of it. Another, older man was leaning forward,
braced with his arms on his thighs, while a third
man sat in a cushioned chair covered with dark
gold vinyl. In the corner of the room near the
couch, a chipped enamel coffee urn sat atop a
table surrounded by cups in assorted shapes and
sizes, as well as a stack of Styrofoam cups.
There was also a container of sugar and a
powdered cream substitute with a couple of
community spoons.

Two doors opened into the long room. One of
them was ajar, giving Shannon a glimpse of
another room that more closely resembled an
office than this one.

All three of the men were staring at her with
open speculation. Shannon had the impression
that it wasn't every day a female invaded their
domain. The older man in the red plaid flannel
shirt finally straightened to his feet. Age had
thickened his figure somewhat without taking
away from his muscled physique. His tanned
face was craggy but pleasant, for some reason

reminding Shannon of a stuffed teddy bear. His dark hair was graying, giving him a grizzled look, but there was a gentle quality in his blue eyes.

"Can I help you, miss?" he inquired in a gruff voice that Shannon instantly recognized. This was the same man she had spoken to on the telephone.

"Yes. My name is Shannon Hayes. I talked to you a little while ago—inquiring about a pilot named Rick Farris," she explained, and noticed the man's eyebrow shoot up.

"I remember, but like I told you, miss, we don't have anybody here by that name." He repeated his previous answer with a show of patience.

"I know you did, but—" she paused to reach inside her purse for Rick's letter "—I just flew into Anchorage this afternoon. I'm trying to locate Rick. He's my fiancé. I received this letter from him indicating that he planned to go to work here for a man named—" she got the letter out to recheck the name "—Cody Steele. I understand he is the owner, is that right?"

"Half-right. Cody and I are partners," he rasped out the correction. "It doesn't really matter what he wrote you, miss. I'd know if we had anybody working for us by that name—and we don't."

"I'm sure you would know if Rick was working for you," Shannon agreed with that. "I was wondering if you might know where he is. Evidently Rick talked to this Cody Steele. Is he in? Could I speak to him?"

"I don't know what good it will do you," he shrugged. "He probably won't remember any more about this fella than I do." He saw that she was going to insist on finding that out for herself, and grimaced his resignment. "But you can ask him."

Turning, he walked to the door standing ajar and pushed it open. Shannon had a glimpse of a lean, dark-haired man poring over papers on his desk. He glanced up at the interruption, cloaked in an attitude of extreme fatigue.

"Yes?" The weary edge to the man's voice asked for an explanation of the disturbance.

"Remember that phone call I got a few minutes ago, Cody?" the older man said. "Well, the lady is here—a cheechako. She wants to talk to you."

Shannon heard a sound like a long sigh, then the creak of a swivel chair being rocked back. The man in the office was lost from her view, blocked by the older and broader figure in the doorway.

"Send her in," was the reply.

The older man stepped out of the way and motioned her inside the office. "He'll see you."

As she walked in, her gaze first noted how neat and orderly the office was compared to the outer room. Then her attention centered on the man behind the desk. He was rubbing a hand over his eyes, a gesture indicative of the tiredness she'd sensed before. The rubbing motion carried his hand to the back of his neck in an effort to ease its weary tension.

At that moment his glance fell on her, and a stillness held him in that position for the span of several seconds. Pitch-black hair framed his lean, sun-hardened features. His eyes were a shade of blue too light for his complexion, which gave an unusual intensity to his gaze. Shannon felt it penetrating her, probing with steady insistence.

In the blink of an eye he seemed to shrug off the tiredness and take on an air of crisp male vitality. There was a certain boldness in the way he looked at her as he swung to his feet, all six-plus feet of him. Working at the desk, he had appeared to be in his late thirties, but Shannon was revising the estimate backward now. He seemed much younger, although still very mature and experienced. She felt the thrust of his male vigor affecting her senses, heightening them in a responsive awareness of him as an attractive member of the opposite sex. It was a natural reaction that didn't disturb her.

"I'm Cody Steele." He extended his hand to her in greeting. The action stretched the heavy knitted pullover sweater across the breadth of his shoulders, its dark charcoal color blending with khaki gray slacks.

"Shannon Hayes." She shook his hand, liking the firmness of his grip.

His all-encompassing gaze had made a very

thorough inspection of her, taking in all her feminine attributes. She doubted if his measuring look had missed anything, yet there had been nothing offensive about it. Shannon wondered why it was that some people could look upon a nude form with an expression that would make it appear to be an object of vulgarity, while others looked at nudity and revealed an appreciation for beauty in its natural form. Some men could undress her with their eyes and make her feel dirty and ashamed; and others, like Cody Steele, could look and make her feel proud of being a woman. She didn't understand the reason for the difference, but it existed.

"Won't you sit down, Miss Hayes?" His voice had a husky pitch to it that was pleasing to the ear. He motioned toward a captain-styled chair in front of his desk.

"Thank you." She lowered herself onto the padded seat while he continued to stand behind the desk.

"Would you like a cup of coffee?" he offered.

Until that moment Shannon hadn't felt the need for any kind of stimulation, caffeine or otherwise. Now it sounded good. "Yes, please."

"Cream? Sugar?"

"Sugar," she admitted.

A plain white cup was sitting on his desk. He picked it up and walked to the door standing ajar to the outer room. Cody Steele paused in its frame. "Dad? Miss Hayes would like a cup of coffee. . . with sugar. I'll have one, too."

Dad? Recognition dawned in her eyes when the older man in the red plaid shirt took the empty cup from Cody's hand and disappeared in the direction of the coffee urn. They were father and son—partners. There was a resemblance, although Cody Steele's features weren't nearly as craggy as his father's, and he was taller and slimmer.

As Cody Steele turned to walk back to the desk while his father brought the coffee, his glance fell on the envelope Shannon was holding. The corners of his mouth were lifted to form a curving line, but there was a certain professionalism to his expression, veiling his male interest in her. At the desk he stopped to set a hip on the edge of it, one leg bent at the knee, and faced her.

"How can I help you, Miss Hayes?" he inquired.

"I'm trying to locate a pilot named Rick Farris. I received this letter from him nearly a month ago." Shannon indicated the envelope in her hand. "From what he wrote, I had the impression he was employed by you."

"I believe my father already told you that we don't have anyone flying for us by that name." He exhibited the same patience his father had displayed toward her inquiry.

"Yes, I know," she admitted. "But Rick must have applied for a position with you. He wouldn't have written what he did if he hadn't had some contact with you."

A question glinted in his light blue eyes, a gleam of curiosity showing, but his father appeared then with the coffee, momentarily interrupting the conversation. Cody Steele waited until the cups had been set on the desk top.

"Offhand I don't recall the name, but I've talked to a lot of people in the past month or so, clients and pilots." There was an expressive lift of his wide shoulders that admitted the possibility he had spoken to Rick. "Do you mind my asking why you are so anxious to locate this man? Is he a relative?"

"He's her fiancé," his father answered for Shannon, and there seemed to be a warning in the look he gave Cody Steele, as if instructing him to behave himself.

There was a flash of indulgent humor in the light blue eyes, although they quickly narrowed slightly when they rested on Shannon. His gaze swung to the letter and envelope in her hand.

"What about the return address on the letter?" he asked.

"I went to the apartment," she admitted. "The manager hasn't seen him in two weeks. Rick left one day and didn't come back." Shannon tried to sound very matter-of-fact, but she heard the note of apprehension creep into her voice.

Cody Steele looked away, letting his attention focus on the cup of coffee he had picked up and allowing her the opportunity to take a firmer grip on her composure. When he spoke, it was to his father. "Close the door on your way out, dad."

His father cast a disapproving glance over his shoulder, but shut the door as he left. Shannon was in control of her nerves when she met the blue eyes again.

"Perhaps if you described your...fiancé to me," Cody Steele suggested.

"He's about your height, with sandy hair and hazel eyes." She reached inside her purse for her wallet and the picture of Rick it contained. Removing the photograph from its plastic holder, she passed it to Cody.

He studied it, then flicked a considering glance at her. "His flying experience?" Dark brows were drawn together in a thoughtful frown.

"He's fully qualified. He has all his ratings." Before she could continue, he nodded his head.

"Yes, I remember talking to him." He returned the photo. "He had been an instructor for six months prior to coming here."

"Yes, that's right." She smiled, relief showing in the faint dimples that dented her cheeks.

"You're from Texas," Cody guessed. "Your... fiancé was, too, as I recall."

"Yes." Her smile widened. There was a responding glint of humor in his eyes. It intensified the inherent boldness that marked him.

"You needn't worry. We Alaskans don't brag

about how big the state is. We just pride our-
selves on being unique.''

The sparkle of wicked amusement was deliberately obvious. Then he added, more
seriously, ''I remember that your fiancé stopped
by to inquire about a position with us, but we
couldn't use him. I wish I could be of more help
than that.''

''Did he indicate where he could be reached?''
Shannon persisted. ''Or where he might be
working?''

''He might have, but to tell you the truth, I
didn't bother to keep his address. Our business
is mainly cross-country charters. Despite his
qualifications, he had no experience flying in
Alaska, so I wasn't interested.''

She was slightly stunned by this definite rejec-
tion of Rick's flying experience. Worse, she
seemed to be faced with another dead end. As if
sensing her dazed reaction, Cody handed her the
cup of coffee. She sipped at the sugared liquid,
then sighed deeply.

''I don't know where to go from here,'' she
murmured in confusion. ''How can I find
him?''

''I suppose you could start calling other flying
services.'' But his tone didn't sound too promis-
ing about her success. ''Maybe he's given up
and gone home. It's possible you wasted your
time coming all the way up here.''

''Rick knew I was coming.'' She shook her
head, refusing to believe his implication. ''He

was expecting me, so he wouldn't have left, not without letting me know. I talked to my parents in Houston just a little while ago. They haven't heard from him."

"How long have you been engaged?"

She didn't see the point to his question, but she answered it anyway. "A year."

"And how long has Rick been here in Alaska?"

"Six months. Why?" She suddenly challenged these questions that seemed to be delving into her personal life.

"You haven't seen him in six months. And you obviously haven't heard from him since you received that letter a month ago. Maybe he's had a change of heart," Cody reasoned.

"No. That isn't possible." Shannon denied that suggestion emphatically.

"Why?" He sounded curious more than anything else.

"Because two weeks ago he sent me a one-way plane ticket to Anchorage. Before he left Houston we agreed that as soon as he found a permanent job and a place for us to live he would send for me." She returned his steady look. "Rick hasn't changed his mind, or he wouldn't have sent the plane fare."

"That doesn't explain why he moved two weeks ago without letting you know," he reminded her.

"I'm...not sure that he moved." Shannon finally voiced the concern that had been on her mind since she'd left Rick's former apartment building. "He left some of his things in his apartment, some clothes and other things, including my picture. If he was moving to another place, why didn't he take all of his belongings?"

He raised an eyebrow at the question and avoided her look as he sipped at his coffee. "He said nothing to his landlord?"

"Just that he'd be back in a couple of days—before the rent was due." Worry gnawed at her. She tried to reason it aside. "I keep telling myself that it's all a mix-up. My telegram went to the apartment, so Rick doesn't even know I'm here in Alaska. Now I don't know where he is or where he's working. If he moved I'm certain he would let me know his new address, because he knew I was coming any day."

"There is probably a simple reason." He shrugged to indicate his lack of concern. "Perhaps he sent you his new address and the letter was lost in the mail. It *has* happened."

"That's true." That hadn't occurred to Shannon, and she breathed a little easier at the thought. "Of course, that doesn't solve the problem of how I'm going to find him."

"Where are you staying?" He half turned to pick up a pen and find a clean slip of paper.

"At the Westward." She watched him jot down the information.

"Why don't you let me check a few places, ask some questions," he suggested. "I'll let you know what I find out, if anything."

"I would be grateful, Mr. Steele." Her smile was small but warmly sincere.

"I'm counting on that, Texas," he replied with a mildly roguish smile, turning her home state into a nickname. "And the name is Cody."

"Thank you...Cody." It was strange how easily she spoke his name. It seemed she had known him prior to this first meeting.

There was a loud knock at the door. "Yes?" Cody turned his head in that direction.

The door opened and the stockier build of Cody's father appeared. "I was just checking to see if you wanted some more coffee." His sharp gaze darted from his son to Shannon, bright with suspicion and revealing surprise that there seemed to be no reason for it.

"Not for me," Cody replied, and glanced at her.

"No, thank you," she refused, and slipped the strap of her purse over her shoulder. "I've taken enough of your time. I'd better be leaving."

"It's still raining out there," his father advised.

"May I use your phone to call a cab?" Shannon requested as she rose to her feet.

Cody straightened from the desk to stand beside her. She was conscious of the warm male smell of him, elusive yet stimulating. Even with the added height of her boots, the top of her head still only reached his chin. At close quarters she was even more conscious of his sexual attraction. She had learned long ago that it was normal for an attractive male to arouse her interest, so she wasn't uncomfortable with the discovery that she found Cody Steele attractive. It had no effect on the way she felt about Rick.

"There's no need for you to call a cab," Cody stated. "I have an appointment downtown. You're welcome to ride with me."

"Thank you. I—" Shannon didn't have a chance to finish her acceptance of his offer.

"What appointment?" his father wanted to know. "You didn't mention anything to me about it. Who do you have to see?"

"I'm going to see Darryl Akers at the bank." Cody appeared to shrug away the importance of his meeting.

"If you're going to the bank, I'd better come along with you," his father stated. "I'll get my coat."

"There's no reason for you to come with me." But Cody was talking to an empty doorway. There was a grim dryness in the glance he slid in Shannon's direction. Then a glint of humor appeared to lighten the blue color of his eyes.

"Parents," he mocked affectionately. "They never listen."

"True." The corners of her mouth deepened with a contained smile, and his gaze observed the action, lingering for a pulse beat on the curve of her lower lip.

"How about that ride, Texas?" he asked.

"Yes," she nodded, the chestnut length of her hair sweeping her shoulders.

"My car is parked outside the building." He let the flat of his hand rest on the small of her back to usher her out of the office. There was a certain ease in the action that had a familiar quality, much too natural to raise any objection from Shannon.

His father was zipping the front of a light jacket as they entered the outer office. He reached the door ahead of them and held it open for Shannon. Cody's hand remained on the back of her waist to guide her, but his father was leading the way toward a late-model car parked in front of the building. He reached it first and opened a rear door, stepping aside so Shannon could slide in.

Cody forestalled her. "Why don't you let Miss Hayes sit in the front seat, dad?" he prompted his father, a thin edge of irritation creeping into his voice.

"I'd look pretty silly sitting in the back seat all by myself after we leave her at the hotel, now, wouldn't I?" his father reasoned.

"You could always move to the front seat," Cody replied.

"What's the point in getting in, then getting out and getting in again?" his father argued, being deliberately difficult.

Shannon settled the disagreement. "I don't

mind sitting in the back seat." She moved to take her place in the back.

"There, you see?" Cody's father beamed in triumph that he'd got his way. "She may be a cheechako, but she's not dumb. She has better sense than to stand around arguing about where she's going to sit when it's raining."

Cody made no reply as he saw Shannon safely inside, but his blue eyes were very expressive of his feelings when they met her glance. He was both irritated and amused by his father's maneuvering. Although she didn't understand the reason behind it, Cody obviously did.

When both men were in the car, Shannon asked, "What does *cheechako* mean?" It was the second time his father had used the term to describe her.

"It refers to a greenhorn or a tenderfoot," Cody explained. "Quite often it's applied to anyone from the outside."

"Outside?" she questioned.

"Anyplace outside of Alaska."

It was a short drive to the hotel. His father began a monologue that lasted until they arrived, eliminating any exchange of conversation during the ride. Before Shannon climbed out of the car, Cody turned to look back over the seat.

"I'll be in touch later to let you know what I've found out," he said.

"All right." She stepped out of the car.

"Found out about what?" his father wanted to know as she shut the rear door. He continued his demand to find out what Cody was talking about, but she didn't actually hear the questions. She waved her thanks for the ride and noticed the tinge of exasperation in Cody's features at his father's incessant prying. Smiling to herself, she walked to the revolving entrance doors to the hotel.

The smile faded when she reached her hotel room. The boxes containing Rick's belongings were sitting beside her luggage. The sight of them started her wondering again where Rick was. Kneeling beside the boxes, she began going through them, looking for any clue—no matter how slim—that might tell her something.

CHAPTER THREE

SHANNON HAD FOUND NOTHING in the boxes, not even a matchbook cover that might tell her of a restaurant or bar that Rick frequented in Anchorage. With the boxes repacked and stored in the hotel closet, she unpacked her suitcases.

Her wedding outfit was a white tailored suit with a ruffled silk blouse of the palest blue and shoes to match. A white pillbox hat with a half veil was her mother's—"something borrowed." Shannon's father had given her an antique brooch that had belonged to his mother, which was to be her "something old."

As she smoothed the lapel of the white jacket, Shannon wondered if there would be a wedding on Saturday. So far she was a bride without a groom. She jumped at the sound of the telephone ringing, her heart catapulting into her throat. Was it Rick?

She nearly tripped over an empty suitcase in her haste to reach the orange telephone on the bedside table. "Hello?" Her voice was eager and expectant, anticipating Rick on the other end.

"Hi, Texas," a husky male voice responded, but it wasn't Rick. "Have you had dinner yet?"

Pausing, she tried to contain her disappointment, but some of it slipped through. "Hello, Cody. No, I haven't. I've been unpacking and...." Suddenly she remembered why he was calling. "Have you found out anything about Rick?"

"Not exactly," he replied.

Which was a definite no. "What did you find out?"

"Mostly I found out where he isn't. I'll tell you all about it over dinner," he said.

"All right. I...." Shannon stopped as she realized she had just accepted his invitation. She hardly knew the man.

"I'll meet you at the restaurant on the top floor of the hotel in... twenty minutes."

There was a click on the line as the connection was broken, before she could decide whether she should meet him or not. She chewed at her lower lip, considering the alternatives. Since he had suggested dining at the hotel, where she would have eaten anyway, it didn't seem to make much difference. It was simply a matter of having company or eating alone. Shannon decided that she preferred company.

Twenty minutes didn't give her much time. Rather than completely changing clothes, she took off her cable-knit pullover to wear just the lavender blouse with the plaid skirt. She slipped off her boots in favor of high-heeled sandals. The addition of an amethyst pendant and drop earrings completed the change as she swept her hair behind her ears, securing it in place with combs.

When she stepped into the elevator and pushed the button for the restaurant on the top floor, Shannon had five minutes to spare. The top floor of the hotel contained a restaurant and lounge. Its glassed walls provided a view of downtown Anchorage and the harbor of Cook Inlet. Leaving the elevator, Shannon paused at the entrance to the restaurant and lounge to look around for Cody.

He was sitting at the bar. When he saw her, he crushed out the cigarette he was smoking and rose to join her at the archway. She noticed he'd changed clothes since she'd last seen him that afternoon. In place of the sweater and slacks he was wearing a navy tweed sports jacket and navy slacks, but no tie. His white dress shirt was open at the throat, exposing the tanned hollow at its base. The lazy charm of his half smile and the admiring light in his blue eyes reached out to draw her into the spell of his vital, sensual presence. Secure in the knowledge of her love for Rick, Shannon didn't feel threatened by it.

"I like it when dinner companions arrive on time," Cody stated with half-mocking approval. "Cooling my heels on an empty stomach isn't a pleasant way to pass the time. Are you hungry?"

"I honestly haven't thought about it," she admitted. "Too many other things on my mind, I guess." Namely, locating Rick.

"When did you eat last?" he prodded her memory.

"This morning on the plane."

"Take my word for it, you're hungry," he stated, and turned to face the hostess as she approached them.

"Two for dinner?" she inquired.

"Yes," Cody affirmed. "We'd like a table by the window, please."

"One moment, please." The woman paused to check the seating-and-reservation chart before showing them to a table.

A gruffly accusing voice came from behind them. "There you are, Cody. I've been looking all over for you." They both turned simultaneously to be confronted by Cody's father. "I recognized your car in the lot across the street and wondered what it was doing there."

"Now you know." There was an underlying hardness to Cody's reply that politely and respectfully suggested his father should get lost.

But the older man stubbornly ignored the broad hint. "I thought I'd check to see what you wanted for dinner tonight before I stopped at the market." Then he shifted his attention to Shannon. "Have you found your fiancé yet?"

"Not yet." She shook her head briefly as a twinge of uncertainty quivered through her at Rick's seeming disappearance.

An arm curved itself along the back of her waist, asserting possession. There was a measure of reassurance in the firm warmth of its pressure. Shannon lifted her gaze to Cody's profile, more smoothly chiseled than his father's craggy features.

"Miss Hayes and I are having dinner tonight, so you can fix what you like," Cody informed him.

"If that's the case, I'd better join the two of you," his father declared. Shannon felt Cody stiffen in resistance, the line of his jaw hardening.

"Dad—" He attempted a protest but wasn't permitted to finish it.

"People might get the wrong impression if they find out you're having dinner with Miss Hayes when she's engaged to somebody else," his father explained his reasoning. "I don't want them to think you are trying to steal her away from her fiancé."

Cody's chest rose in a deep breath, which he expelled as a sigh. His glance sliced to the hostess. "Change that to a table for three," he requested grimly.

Concealing a smile, Shannon followed the hostess to a table set for four by the window. She was beginning to get the feeling that Cody's father didn't exactly trust his son to behave "properly" with her. He was appointing himself as chaperon to make certain Cody did. It was both touching and amusing to have her reputation so staunchly protected. Shannon wasn't sure whether the elder Steele believed females were too weak to know their own minds or whether he believed Cody was irresistible.

After Cody had seated her in the chair closest to the window, he took the one beside her, facing his father across the table. She pretended not to notice the exchange of warring glances as she studied the view out the window. Clouds continued to blanket the sky, but it had stopped raining, the visibility improving.

"The ceiling has lifted some," Cody remarked, using the aeronautical term to refer to the higher cloud cover. "You can see a bit farther than you could earlier today."

"That bay is Cook Inlet, isn't it?" Shannon guessed.

"That's right," Mr. Steele answered. "Sometimes there's as much as a twenty-nine-foot difference in the tides."

Shannon looked suitably impressed, then let her gaze swing to the range of mountains rising inland to wall in the city. The gathering shadows of twilight made them indistinct. Streetlights were blinking on in anticipation of the coming nightfall.

"On a clear day you can see the twin peaks of Mount McKinley, roughly a hundred and fifty miles north," Cody told her. "It's the highest mountain on the continent. At twenty-thousand-plus feet, it's the third highest in the world. Aconcagua in Argentina is the second highest, and there's a hill called Everest over in the Himalayas that *claims* to be the highest."

Catching the mocking emphasis on the word, she glanced at the man seated next to her. The gleam of dancing amusement sharpened the blue of his eyes, his rough-cut features lazy with humor. It was impossible not to be drawn into his light mood.

"It only *claims* to be?" Amused, she questioned his choice of words, the sparkle of laughter in her brown eyes.

"It cheats," Cody replied, the corners of his mouth deepening without an acutal smile showing.

Shannon laughed in her throat. "How does it do that?"

"Very easily. It rises from a plateau that's already at fourteen thousand feet, which gives it quite a head start. The land at the base of McKinley has an elevation of some three thousand feet and the mountain rises seventeen thousand feet from there. Now, if we just discount the fact that Mount Aconcagua exists, then Alaska rightfully has the highest mountain in the world," he concluded.

Shannon laughed. "But you're not bragging," she countered with a mocking twinkle lighting her eyes.

"Texas, we don't brag," Cody chided, a smile slowly widening his mouth, warmly mocking and captivating in its effect.

With difficulty Shannon broke contact with his gaze when the waitress stopped at their table. "Would any of you care for cocktails before dinner?" she inquired.

"Nothing for me, thank you," Shannon refused, and opened the menu lying in front of her.

Neither Cody nor his father ordered a drink, either. The waitress left to give them a few minutes to peruse the menu and returned later to take their order. On Cody's recommendation, Shannon chose the broiled salmon steak with cream-of-celery soup as a starter. Both men opted for steak and salad.

As she passed the menu back to the waitress, Shannon was aware that Cody had casually stretched his right arm across the top of her chair back. There wasn't any actual physical contact, but his father eyed the move with obvious disapproval.

"That is a beautiful engagement ring, Miss Hayes." He reached across the table and lifted her left hand as if to make a closer inspection of the ring, slicing a sharp look at Cody, who had leaned back in his chair and was idly rubbing a forefinger across his mouth. "Did you notice it, Cody?" he asked pointedly.

"Yes, dad. As a matter of fact, I did," Cody admitted with a mildly sardonic smile.

"Yes, sir, it's a beautiful ring," his father repeated as he released her hand.

Shannon was vaguely amused at the way his father was so determined to impress on Cody that she wasn't available. "Thank you, Mr. Steele," she responded to the compliment.

"Call me Noah. Everyone does," he insisted. "When's the wedding?"

"Saturday. At least, that's what we had planned." She quickly qualified her initial answer. Concern for Rick sobered her expression as her questioning glance swung to Cody. "What did you find out today? About Rick?"

He stopped rubbing his bent forefinger across his mouth and lowered his arm to the table, absently straightening the silverware. "I found out where he isn't."

"Where is that?" she asked.

"He isn't a patient at any of the local hospitals—or in jail." His emotionless tone caused Shannon to stiffen in recognition of a possibility she had been afraid to consider. His side-glance caught her movement, and he went on to explain, "There was a chance that he could have become ill or been in an accident, but no one by that name, nor anyone fitting his description, has been admitted to the hospital in the past three weeks. The police have no record on him, either."

"I should be relieved to know he isn't sick or injured," she murmured with a troubled sigh.

"But it's all the more confusing. A person just can't disappear. . . without a trace."

"At least you can rest easy that he's safe and unharmed." Noah Steele insisted that she should be comforted by the knowledge.

"Don't misunderstand. I'm glad Rick is all right. It's just that I'm no closer to finding him than I was before." Her voice was weighted with the frustration and confusion she felt.

"You haven't had much time to look, either," Cody reminded her calmly. "You only arrived in Anchorage this afternoon."

"It seems much longer." She grimaced wryly.

"You must be exhausted after all that traveling," Noah Steele declared in sympathy. "You need a good night's rest, so don't let Cody keep you up till all hours talking. Once you've had dinner, you should go straight to your room."

"I have no intention of keeping Miss Hayes up late tonight." Even when he was irritated with his father, there was a strong thread of respect and affection in Cody's voice, Shannon noticed.

"I should hope not," his father returned. "You belong in bed yourself." Then he explained to Shannon, "Cody just got back this afternoon from flying some freight to Dutch Harbor in the Aleutians, which is quite a trek. In his line of work he has to be alert and on his toes at all times, which means he needs plenty of rest."

She recalled how tired he had seemed at the

Steele Air office, although it was difficult to detect any weariness in him now. There was a resiliency about his strength, a whipcord durability that encouraged others to depend on him—the way she was doing.

"Your concern is touching, dad," Cody murmured dryly, and paused as the waitress arrived with their first course. When it was served he removed his arm from her chair back, letting his glance touch her with its light intensity. "It's amazing how food and sleep can improve a person's outlook. The situation won't seem quite as bleak to you in the morning."

"Probably not," she agreed as she thoughtfully stirred her soup. "I have one definite clue. Rick has a job, otherwise he wouldn't have sent me that plane ticket. Tomorrow I'll start calling all the flying companies until I find the one where he's employed." She paused, a tiny frown of confusion making faint lines on her forehead. "Why did Rick have such a hard time finding a job when he's so well qualified?"

"His lack of experience," Cody replied.

His father elaborated. "Conditions here aren't the same as he's used to on the outside. Anchorage, Fairbanks, Juneau, they all have fully equipped, modern airports, as good as any you'll find in the smaller states. But once you're out in the bush, your airstrip might turn out to be a sandbar along some river. And no radar or sophisticated navigational gear is going to find it for you. From the air it's hard to tell one river and mountain from another, especially in the spring, when creeks become rivers. I've been a bush pilot for thirty-five years and there have been times when I've been lost. If you make a mistake in this country, you don't often get a chance to make another one. It's no place for a cheechako.''

"I'm beginning to understand," she murmured. Which was true. She had a much clearer understanding of what had appealed to Rick. It was the danger, as well as the challenge and excitement of a new frontier.

Her glance strayed to Cody, reassessing him. Rick's letter had been filled with glowing praise for this man's ability. Behind that reckless smile and those bold eyes there was a swift, calculating mind, always weighing odds and chances and making split-second decisions. If he ever took chances, they were deliberate ones—with all factors taken into consideration beforehand.

"You take Cody here," Noah Steele continued. "He's been flying since his legs were long enough to reach the rudder pedals. It's nothing for a boy to learn to fly before he learns to drive a car out here. Half the roads in Alaska don't go anywhere, leastwise rarely to the place you want to go. I taught Cody everything he knows. There's some would argue, but he's the best in the business as far as I'm concerned.''

"You understand he's a little prejudiced,''

Cody murmured in an aside to her that was dryly mocking.

"I am prejudiced, but facts are facts," Noah
defended his claim. "I've seen a lot of hotshot
pilots in my day—air-force jet jockeys and commercial pilots. When they're redlining a plane
they're in a cold sweat."

"Anything below or above the maximum and
minimum recommended by the aircraft manu-
facturer as safe operating limits is referred to as
'red line,'" Cody explained the term.

"He knows the limits of his aircraft," his
father assured her. "He pushes it to that point
and no further. That's why he's sitting here
tonight when some others didn't make it. He
knows what he's doing every minute."

Noah stopped abruptly, as if just discovering
he'd said something profound. He eyed his son
sharply, then glanced at Shannon. "I shouldn't
have rattled on like that. You'll just have to
mark it off as a father's pride. I know you
aren't interested in hearing about Cody now
when you're so anxious about your fiancé."

She sensed his underlying regret that he'd
talked so much about his son, perhaps raising
her estimation of Cody over that of Rick. He
had included himself at the table to keep the two
of them apart, she realized, not to interest Shannon in his son.

"I'm interested in what is entailed in being a
bush pilot," she insisted. "After all, it's the
profession Rick is seeking, so I should know

something about it." Noah Steele looked relieved by her reply, satisfied that he hadn't committed a terrible blunder by talking at such length about his son and flying. "I have to confess I don't know very much about Alaska."

"Except that it's bigger than Texas," Cody prompted with a teasing inflection."

"I've heard that rumor." An answering smile played with the corners of her mouth.

"If you take Alaska at its widest point," his father spoke up, "and put one end in Maine, the other end would reach to San Diego."

She looked at him in faint astonishment. "Are you serious?"

"The Aleutian chain of islands alone is more than a thousand miles long," Noah pointed out. "This is the only state with four time zones within its boundaries, which should give you some idea of its size."

"But he's not bragging," Cody inserted with a quirking smile.

Unaware of their private joke, his father insisted, "It's a fact. I'm not exaggerating."

"I'm impressed," Shannon said, and meant it.

"People on the outside have a lot of misconceptions about Alaska," Noah remarked. "Generally they associate the name with cold weather, Eskimos and dog sleds."

"Not to mention the 'Texas tea' that was found at a little place called Prudhoe Bay on the North Slope," Cody murmured dryly, in reference to the Alaskan oil discovery.

"I'd heard rumors to the effect that you'd found a little crude," she countered, finally aware that it was a vast understatement.

"I still haven't made up my mind whether that was a good thing or not for Alaska," Cody's father declared in a contemplative fashion.

There was a break in the conversation as the waitress served their entrée. Afterward Noah resumed his discussion of the changes that had come about in Alaska since the oil discovery and the subsequent construction of the trans-Alaska pipeline. A few interested questions from Shannon encouraged the garrulous man to expound his opinions. The topic continued through the meal, finally lagging over the second cup of coffee.

During a moment of quiet, Shannon was caught smothering a yawn with her hand. "The jet lag has finally caught up with you," Noah Steele announced. "It's time you were calling it a night."

"It's early yet." Her watch indicated that, but it was set according to this time zone. Her system hadn't made the adjustment yet.

"Dad's right." Cody surprised his father with his agreement, and pushed his chair away from the table to stand and assist Shannon. "It's time you were turning in." His hand cupped her elbow, firm in its grip. "I'll see you to your room," he stated. There was a complacent gleam in his eyes when he met his father's startled look. "Take care of the check, will you, dad? I'll meet you downstairs in the lobby."

Before his father could stammer a protest, Cody was guiding Shannon away from the table. A sideways glance noticed the smile that lurked at the edges of his mouth. Sensing her gaze, Cody glanced down at her, and the suggestion of a smile became more evident.

"What self-respecting man would want his father with him when he walked a beautiful woman to her door?" Cody asked in defense of his bit of maneuvering to be alone with her. The glint in his eye showed he viewed the situation in a humorous light, insisting Shannon should do the same. She was beginning to realize that Cody rarely treated anything too seriously—at least not on the surface.

"I am engaged," she replied in a tone that laughingly prodded him.

He winced in a feigned grimace. "Please don't remind me." He punched the button for the elevator, and a set of doors obligingly opened, without making them wait. Once they were inside, the doors closed and Cody pushed her floor number.

"Your father is a remarkable man," she said as they began their descent. "I like him."

"So do I, but don't tell him that," he grinned. "Ignoring the fact that he's my father, he's also the best pilot I've ever known."

"Does he still fly?"

"He was grounded this spring—couldn't pass his medical," Cody explained with a grim lift of his mouth. "He hasn't quite figured out what to do with himself yet, which is why he tends to get himself involved in matters that don't concern him."

Like this evening, appointing himself as her chaperon, Shannon thought. The elevator stopped on her floor. Cody's hand was at the back of her waist, providing unobtrusive guidance as they started down the hotel corridor.

"He's become my self-appointed guardian, determined to keep me out of trouble." His glance swept over her face. "It's difficult to tell him to butt out of my personal life without hurting his feelings."

"I imagine it would be. It can't be easy for either of you," she sympathized.

"Don't feel sorry for him. He's as cagey as a wolf and five times as smart," Cody assured her.

She paused in front of the door to her hotel room to extract the key from her purse, and glanced at him through the sweep of her lashes. "Like father, like son?" she guessed.

There was a hint of a smile, but Cody didn't respond as he took the key from her and unlocked the door, pushing it open. He pressed the key into her left palm and held onto her hand, turning it over to study the diamond ring on her finger. His attention drew Shannon's gaze to it.

"You're really going to marry this guy when you find him?" His remark seemed to challenge her.

Her head moved in a nod as she stared at the ring Rick had placed on her finger. "My parents were going to fly here this weekend for the wedding, but we may not be able to make the necessary arrangements in time. It's possible we'll have to postpone the ceremony until next Saturday," she conceded.

His hand cupped her cheek and jaw, forcing Shannon to lift her chin and look at him. The disturbing intensity of his gaze held her attention while his thumb rubbed her cheekbone in an absent caress.

"You say it's been six months since you've seen him?" his low voice was challenging.

"Six months," Shannon admitted, aware of the quickening rush of blood through her veins.

His thumb slid down to trace the outline of her lips while his light blue eyes studied the action. "Six months without a man's caress," he mused. "For six months these lips haven't been kissed. That's a crime."

His head bent to bring his mouth against them. A sense of loyalty to Rick kept Shannon motionless beneath the warm pressure as his mouth moved over her lips with sensually exploring ease. The kiss made no demand for a response, but she realized that six months of

abstinence had made her hungry for the touch
of a man, not just that of her fiancé. She was
enjoying the feel of his mouth against hers, the
male smell of him filling her lungs.

If he had wanted to, Cody could have over-
come her passivity and aroused a response, but
he pulled slowly away. Shannon believed it was
out of deference to her engaged status, but she
wasn't sure. She should have felt relieved that
he hadn't pressed home his advantage, but instead she felt vaguely disappointed.

Satisfaction glinted in his look when he
surveyed her upturned face. "Don't mention
this kiss to dad, will you?" he said. "If he
found out about this innocent little kiss, he'd
probably take a belt to me."

He was dismissing the kiss as being of no importance, which was the way she had decided to
regard it. So why was she sorry that he considered it to be insignificant? Was it ego? The
desire to conquer even if she wasn't interested in
the victory? It troubled her that she wasn't
treating the kiss as casually as it should be
treated.

"It will be our secret," she agreed, smiling in
an attempt to make a joke of it.

"Good." He appeared pleased with her
answer. "It's been a long day. You'd better get
some rest. It's time I was heading downstairs—
before dad shows up with a shotgun."

"Thanks for dinner," she remembered as he
moved away from the door.

"I'll be sure to pass the message on to dad," he promised with a saluting wave.

Inside her room, Shannon leaned against the closed door. "This is crazy," she murmured after a second. "If he had kissed me with passion, I would have been outraged. Now, because it was a friendly, innocent kiss, I'm wondering what's wrong with me. He respected me and I'm wishing he hadn't. Oh, Rick," she sighed, and looked at her ring. "Where are you?" she whispered, suddenly desperately needing to see him again.

CHAPTER FOUR

BY MIDAFTERNOON of the following day, the clouds had blown away and the sun had come out to shine its warmth on the city. The tan corduroy blazer was all Shannon needed in the way of a jacket as she wandered aimlessly through the downtown business district.

She'd been on the telephone all morning and the bulk of the afternoon, calling the various charter and flying services to see if Rick was employed there. Some recalled that he had applied for a position, most had no recollection of him at all, and none of them had him listed on their payroll.

A sense of defeat had driven her out of the room to walk off some of her frustration. She kept searching the faces of the people on the off chance that by some miracle she'd find Rick among them. She paused at a crosswalk and glanced around to get her bearings. Across the street was her hotel. She'd come full circle. There was no place else for her to go.

Crossing the street, she entered the hotel through the revolving doors. As she walked through the lobby, she thought she heard someone call her name and stopped to look over her shoulder. Her mouth curved into a smile that didn't lighten the defeated dullness of her eyes.

"Hello, Mr. Steele," she greeted the older man, and half turned as he approached. "I didn't expect to see you today.

"Noah," he corrected.

"Noah," she repeated in acknowledgment. "Is Cody with you?" Her glance made a brief sweep of the lobby in search of his dark-haired son.

"No, he's busy," Noah explained, and Shannon felt a slight letdown at the answer. "I had some free time, so I thought I'd stop by to see if you had any luck finding your boyfriend."

"No." She shook her head, the corners of her mouth drooping. "I called every company in the telephone book. A couple of them remember talking to him, but Rick isn't working for any of them." Her shoulders lifted in an expressive shrug. "I just don't know what to do next."

"Let me buy you a cup of coffee." He winked as if he knew the remedy. "Nothing is ever as bad as it seems."

"That's what I keep telling myself," she sighed, and let herself be led to the coffee shop off the hotel lobby. "At this point I'm open to any suggestion."

"Two coffees," Noah Steele ordered as the uniformed waitress brought glasses of ice water to their table. He waited until she returned with a pot of coffee and the two brown mugs were filled before he responded to her earlier state-ment. "Maybe you should go to the police and file a missing-persons report on him."

"I've been thinking about that." She measured a spoonful of sugar into her coffee and stirred. "Except that I don't know that Rick is missing. I just don't know where he is. I'd feel pretty foolish it if turned out to be a false alarm."

In her side vision she caught a glimpse of a tall figure entering the coffee shop. When the man started walking toward their table, she turned her head to cast a curious glance in his direction. Recognizing Cody, she sent a startled look at his father.

"I thought you said Cody wasn't with you," she said.

A fleeting expression of guilt crossed his features when he looked around to see his son approaching them. "No, he didn't come with me," Noah Steele insisted.

"Hello, Shannon." Cody smiled at her, then turned a speculative look on his father. "Dad, this is a surprise. What are you doing here?"

"I thought I'd stop by to see Miss Hayes and find out whether she'd had any luck locating her fiancé." His features were almost too bland. "After all, she doesn't know a soul here, so it can't be easy on her, being alone with no one to turn to for help."

"Strange," Cody murmured, tipping his head

to one side. "Those words sound very familiar. I believe I expressed a similar thought about an hour ago when you asked me what my plans were tonight."

A redness crept up his father's neck, and Shannon realized Noah had known all along that Cody intended to see her today. That's why he'd arranged to be there first, so Cody would be the one intruding this time. The only problem was that Cody had exposed his father's hand and revealed his intention.

"Why don't you sit down and have a cup of coffee with us?" his father invited.

"Why, thank you," Cody mocked the invitation, pulling an empty chair away from the next table. "Did you have any luck, Texas?"

"No. I called everyone. I don't know where to go from here," she repeated her earlier frustration.

"Maybe he got a job doing something besides flying," Noah Steele suggested.

"No." Shannon was positive about that. "He would have come home before he'd done that. Wherever he's working, you can be sure it's associated with flying. He wouldn't have settled for anything less than that."

"There are any number of companies that have their own fleet of planes." Cody filled an empty cup with coffee from the insulated pot on the table, his remark raising her hopes and offering her another avenue to pursue in her search for Rick. "He could have hired on as a copilot or navigator for one of them, to gain some experience in this kind of country."

"Say, now that's an idea!" his father declared, showing approval of the suggestion. "Wade Rafferty is a good friend of yours. Why don't you check with him?"

Shannon glanced from one to the other, her brown eyes dark with confusion. "Who is Wade Rafferty?" The name meant nothing to her, and certainly not in connection with Rick.

"Wade is Cody's fishing buddy," Noah Steele replied, which meant even less.

"Wade heads up the Alaskan operation of a petroleum company with interests in the pipeline." Cody's explanation made more sense. "He would know or could easily check to see if your fiancé is flying for any of the oil companies."

"Would he?" She was almost holding her breath as her gaze clung to Cody.

"If Cody asked him, I'm sure he'd do it as a personal favor," his father insisted.

"I believe he would," Cody verified his father's statement. Her anxiously eager expression seemed to ask what he was waiting for. He studied it, one corner of his mouth lifting in resignation. Then with a little push he shoved himself away from the table and straightened from his chair. "I'll call him right now."

"Thank you." A glowing smile of gratitude

brought a shine to her features that caught his attention. The light color of his eyes gave an intensity to his look as he searched her face, probing for the source of her emotion. For a brief second he uncovered something. Shannon didn't have a chance to identify the feeling deep inside before some inner mechanism shut it out of her conscious mind, but it left her a little shaken.

A jet-black brow was arched in her direction. "Are you sure you want me to find your fiancé, Texas?" It was a low question, quietly issued.

Before she could clear her muddled thoughts to assert her assurance that she did, Cody's father sharply reprimanded him for the question. "Why did you ask a thing like that? Of course she wants him found! She's going to marry him, for heaven's sake!"

There was an invisible shrug as he relented in his demand for an answer from her. "I'll phone Wade and get the search in motion on his end," he said, excusing himself.

His long, deceptively lazy stride carried him quickly out of her sight toward the public phones in the hotel lobby. Shannon sipped her sweetened coffee with a preoccupied air, her thoughts swelling with Cody and his question, which shouldn't have disturbed her.

As if reading her mind, his father spoke up. "Don't you be letting Cody put doubts in your mind."

"He isn't," she assured him, and thus convinced herself.

"That's a relief." Noah sat back in his chair, relaxing a little. "Once that boy makes up his mind that he wants something, he has the devil's own persuasion to get it. I have my hands full just keeping him in line sometimes."

"Are you hinting that Cody wants me?" There was a thread of amusement in her voice, prompted by his staunch protection of her engaged status.

Noah Steele looked briefly uncomfortable, then bluntly admitted, "He's made it plain that he's attracted to you. I saw it in his face when you walked into the office the other day. I don't want you getting the wrong idea about Cody. He wouldn't make any move unless he had a signal from you that you wouldn't object." Lest she think that he was casting any aspersions on her character, he hastened to assure her, "I don't normally interfere in my son's private matters. It's just that with your fiancé missing and all, you're in a kind of vulnerable position."

"I think I can take care of myself," she suggested gently but firmly.

"Maybe so." He conceded that it was possible she could. "But it seems to me that since your fiancé isn't here to look after his interests, somebody should do it for him. Once we find him, if Cody wants to make a play to win you away from him, then it would all be fair and square."

"I appreciate what you are saying, Mr. Steele. But I hardly know your son—and he barely knows me." Shannon resisted the way he was taking it all so seriously.

There was a determined shake of his head, dismissing her argument. "You can know a person for twenty years and not know him any better than a stranger on the street. Or you can meet a stranger and twenty minutes later feel as though you've known him all your life. Time isn't a measure."

Shannon was forced to agree. Within minutes after meeting Cody, there had been a purely instinctive feeling that she had known him a long time. It was not something that could be explained. But the subject was shunted aside when she saw Cody approaching the table.

Before she could ask whether he had been able to reach his friend, Cody was relaying the results of his phone call.

"I talked to Wade and he's going to check his employee files." Cody sat down in the chair he had vacated earlier. "He suggested that if we stop by his house around seven this evening, he may have some answers for us." His glance stayed with Shannon, not straying to his father.

"That would be nice," Noah endorsed the suggestion. "I haven't seen little Molly in almost a month. I'll bet she's grown an inch."

"Molly is Wade's and Maggie's daughter.

She's two months old," Cody explained for Shannon's benefit.

"Yeah," his father agreed, and elaborated on the explanation. "Molly is Cody's goddaughter."

"Really." Her interested glance ran back to Cody and the glinting blue of his eyes.

"Do you have trouble picturing me as a family man?" It was a low question, with a suggestion of intimacy in its tone.

After only a second's consideration, Shannon shook her head. "No." She was faintly surprised to discover that she didn't have any difficulty visualizing him with children. There was a part of him that was almost boyish, allowing him to play children's games and create new ones. There was also an iron discipline behind those rugged and smiling features that would stand him in good stead as a parent.

"That's good," he murmured, and there was something in his look that sent a hot warmth through her veins.

Shannon attempted to change the subject away from her. "You must have known Wade Rafferty and his wife for a long time."

"Wade and I got acquainted about six years ago when he first came to Alaska." Amusement glittered in his eyes; he was aware of her ploy.

"Almost seven," his father corrected, and Shannon was relieved to have him take part in the conversation again. "We haven't known Maggie, his wife, that long, of course."

"Have they recently married?" she asked.

"You could say that," Noah Steele agreed with a broad hint that there was a great deal more to the story. "You see, they were divorced when Wade moved up here. He went back to Seattle about a year...year and a half ago. It was really an unusual set of circumstances. You see, Wade was engaged to Belinda Hale, the daughter of the president of his firm. He'd gone back to break the news to his son, Mike, and get married. He got married all right, but to his first wife, Maggie." He paused, a grim expression dominating his rough features. "It was too bad about Belinda."

"We won't go into that now, dad." Beneath Cody's casual statement there seemed to be a warning.

His father flashed a look at Shannon and shifted uneasily in his chair. "Yeah, I'm talking out of turn," he admitted.

Shannon idly concluded that Cody didn't feel his father should be gossiping about his friend's personal affairs, and let the curious reference to Belinda Hale go without comment. After all, it had nothing to do with her.

"Where would you like to have dinner tonight, Texas?" Cody asked.

She took a breath, remembering the big meal she'd had the night before, and knew she wasn't hungry enough to eat that much again. "I don't have much of an appetite tonight." She shrugged her indifference to food.

"I'm sure you could eat a sandwich," Cody asserted. "There's an excellent deli up the street."

"We'll eat there," his father stated. "This time Cody can pick up the check."

In spite of herself, Shannon laughed at Noah's insistence that he wasn't going to be stuck with paying for their meals a second night in a row. A surge of gratitude followed at the way this father-and-son pair were keeping her spirits up. Alone, she would have worried herself sick about Rick, but they kept the gloomy shadows at bay.

"Okay, you've talked me into it," she agreed, the soft laughter staying in her voice.

Leaving the coffee shop together, they paused at the cashier's while Noah paid for the coffee. Then it was outside into the crispness of an Alaskan autumn. With a Steele on either side of her to guide her to their destination, Shannon started up the street. At an intersection she spied a word included in a store sign. Its frequent use in store names had earlier aroused her curiosity, which now came to the forefront.

"What is a cache?" she asked her escorts. "So far I've seen shops called a fur cache, a book cache and a jewelry cache."

"'Cache' is an Alaskan term." Cody pronounced it "cash." "It is a small storage building that is elevated on poles to keep animals from reaching it. It was used a lot in rural areas for food storage, and it still is. It's become somewhat a symbol of Alaska.''

"I can see why," Shannon replied. "It's unique."

"Alaska prides itself on being unique," he reminded her with a twinkling glance.

"But you don't brag about being big," she teased him back.

"No, we leave the bragging to that small state down south called Texas." A warmly mocking smile lifted the edges of his mouth. The needling was all done in the name of good fun. Shannon's sense of humor accepted that, and she laughed softly. The comparison of their home states was becoming a private joke between them—something personal and warm.

"Here we are," Noah announced, and stepped forward to open the door to the delicatessen for Shannon.

A hostess showed them to a booth and left them menus. Shannon ordered a roast beef sandwich on a sourdough bun, believing that she was ordering in proportion to her appetite. When it was served, she realized she had been mistaken. Between the bun halves there was a mound of sliced beef, and the bun occupied nearly the entire plate.

"I can't possibly eat all of this," she protested as she viewed the size of the sandwich. "There is enough for three people here."

"You Texans must not have very healthy appetites," Cody chided.

"Not as healthy as you Alaskans have, obviously," she agreed on a laughing note, and added wickedly, "Of course, you burn up a lot of calories keeping warm during your daylong arctic nights."

"We usually find ways to keep warm," he countered suggestively, and Shannon decided against pursuing that line of banter.

Picking up half of the sandwich, she reverted to her original statement. "I'm not going to be able to eat all of this."

"Do the best you can," Noah advised. "You need to keep up your strength. We can't have you wasting away to nothing before your wedding day."

As she bit into her sandwich, she was conscious of Cody glancing at the diamond ring on her finger. She wasn't sure whether it was his father's remark or her engagement ring that caused him to fall silent, but he offered little conversation while they ate. She managed to eat half of the sandwich and force down part of the second half before her stomach protested that it was full and refused to tolerate another bite. As she leaned against the slatted boards forming the booth's backrest, she noticed that Cody also had left a large portion of his sandwich uneaten.

"You didn't have much of an appetite, either, did you?" she observed.

He flashed her a remote blue glance to acknowledge the remark, but did not directly respond to it. Instead he glanced at his watch.

"It's nearly seven. Wade's expecting us." He reached for the bill the waitress had left on the table and slid out of the booth.

His father quickly wiped at his mouth with a napkin and followed suit. "Where did you park your car, Cody?" he asked as he politely helped Shannon out of the booth.

"Across the street from the hotel, near your pickup," Cody answered, and took out his wallet to pay for their meal.

"Good. I'll ride with you and Shannon. When you bring her back to the hotel later on this evening, I can pick up my truck then. That way we can save the gas it would take to drive two vehicles," Noah declared, satisfied that his solution was both logical and practical. Cody offered no objection to the arrangement.

After leaving the delicatessen, they back-tracked their route to the hotel and crossed the street to the parking lot where Cody had left his car. In the business district of Anchorage, neatly painted homes often shared the same block with commercial buildings, but it was to a residential area overlooking the bay that Cody drove them. The side street he took ended in a cul-de-sac, fanned with rustic two-story homes, heavily beamed and sided out of natural stained wood. He parked in the driveway of one of them and shut off the engine.

"It's a beautiful home," Shannon remarked with sincere praise.

Cody directed a half smile at her as he opened

his car door. "Not everyone in Alaska lives in a log cabin or an igloo."

It was almost a relief to have him tease her again about her misformed conceptions of Alaska. He had been much too preoccupied since their evening meal. She had begun to wonder if something was wrong.

Noah opened the front passenger door and extended a hand to help her as she stepped out of the car. "You'll like the Raffertys," he assured her in the gruff voice that masked his extraordinarily gentle nature. "They're a nice family."

A sidewalk curved from the driveway to the front door. Following Cody, Shannon walked ahead of his father to the sheltered stoop of the entry and waited while Cody pushed the button for the doorbell.

The door was opened by a young boy of about twelve with dark hair and eyes and a sprinkling of freckles across the bridge of his nose. He was holding a fussing baby against his shoulder.

"Hiya, Cody." His voice was in the midst of changing octaves as he greeted Cody with easy familiarity. "Come in. Dad is on the telephone and mom's in the kitchen rescuing a cake from the oven. She forgot to set the timer, so it might not be edible."

"Hello, Mike." Cody returned the greeting and stepped to one side to let Shannon enter the house ahead of him. Once she and his father were inside the tiled foyer, he introduced her. "Mike, I'd like you to meet Shannon Hayes. This is Mike Rafferty and his baby sister, Molly."

"Pleased to meet you, Miss Hayes," Mike nodded. His sister began squirming fretfully in his arms.

"I'll hold her," Cody volunteered, and relieved the boy of his wiggling burden without a trace of awkwardness. "How have you been, Molly?" Cody asked, as if he expected an answer. The baby's dark eyes opened wide in an attempt to focus on the face of the man holding her.

"You'd better take this, Cody." Mike passed him a small towel. "She's been spitting up a lot. It really makes your clothes smell if it gets on them." His nose wrinkled in distaste.

"What do you think of my goddaughter, Texas?" Cody asked with a trace of pride.

"She's beautiful." She marveled at the thick mass of curling black hair on the baby's head.

"Molly has her daddy's coloring—black hair and black eyes," Cody remarked absently.

"Yeah, but she's got my mom's temper," Mike declared. "When she gets mad, you can hear her screaming a block away. She's spoiled already."

A woman's voice came from the living room, laughing and warm. "And look who is spoiling her? Every time she whimpers, Mike is there to pick her up!"

Shannon turned to watch the petite, vivacious redhead approach them. "Hello, Cody, Noah. It's good to see you again." Her green eyes swung their curious glance to Shannon. "I'm Maggie Rafferty." She didn't wait for an introduction.

"Shannon Hayes," Shannon volunteered.

"Welcome to Alaska," the redhead responded warmly, then let her smile encompass the others. "Come on in and make yourselves comfortable. Wade knows you're here, so he should be out directly."

A natural stone fireplace dominated the cozy room with its paneled walls and beamed ceiling. Comfortable overstuffed furniture was clustered about the hearth, spaced close for intimate conversations. A thick shag carpet carried out the gold theme of the room, a warm deep color. As Shannon sat down on the opposite end of the short brown-and-gold-patterned sofa from Cody, a tall dark-haired man entered the room from a branching hallway, his broad muscled frame enhanced by a heavily ribbed sweater of smoke gray.

There was a rush of exchanged greetings, and Shannon's introduction to her host, Wade Rafferty. Then there was a moment of calm as Wade joined his red-haired wife on the sofa, a twin to the one on which Cody and Shannon were seated. She watched his arm so naturally circle Maggie's shoulders in a loving gesture of closeness that she momentarily forgot the question she wanted to ask about Rick. The short quiet was broken by the baby in Cody's arms as she began a fussing cry.

"I'll take her." Mike was quick to reach for his little sister. "She probably wants a bottle or something."

As he lifted her out of Cody's arms and started to carry her from the room, Maggie Rafferty spoke up. "Don't let her go to sleep yet, Mike."

"Molly takes after her mother," Wade explained with a mocking glance at his wife. "She has absolutely no respect for time. She has her days and nights mixed up and expects everyone to march to the beat of her drum." Then he smiled at the others. "If I want Maggie to be ready on time for anything, I have to set all the clocks in the house ahead one hour."

"Wade Rafferty, that isn't true!" Maggie denied with mock outrage.

"All right," he conceded. "I only set them a half an hour ahead."

"That's true," Maggie admitted with a laugh.

Cody shifted position on the sofa, stretching his arm along the backrest behind Shannon. Her glance swung to him and met the silent assurance of his gaze. Briefly his hand touched her shoulder.

"I know Shannon is anxious, so I'll ask the question for her," he said. "Were you able to find any leads about her fiancé, Wade?"

There was a slight pause as his coal-dark gaze

rested on her. "Nothing, I'm afraid," he admitted, and dejection drooped her shoulders a fraction of an inch.

"Not a thing?" Shannon echoed softly, and felt the warm clasp of Cody's hand on her shoulder in quiet comfort, a measure of his strength flowing into her.

"No." Wade shook his head and eyed her gently. "I checked the employee files for both the flight crew and the ground crew. There is no one by the name of Farris employed by us. However, I am checking with the other companies in the consortium to see if he might be flying with one of their crews. They promised to get back to me tomorrow. I'm sorry I don't have more information to give you."

She swallowed the lump of disappointment and managed to smile. "I'm truly grateful that you took the trouble to check."

"It wasn't any trouble," he assured her, then attempted to lighten the atmosphere. "Would you mind telling me how you managed to get hooked up with this devil from out of the blue?" he asked, indicating Cody.

"From Rick's last letter, I had the impression he was working for Cody," she explained, and silently decided there was a degree of accuracy in Wade's description of Cody. That wicked glint in his blue eyes had a hint of the devil from out of the blue. "So when Rick wasn't at the airport to meet me and his landlord claimed he'd moved out of his apartment,

I went to Steele Air, thinking I would find Rick there."

"Only he wasn't working for us," Cody carried the explanation further. "I couldn't turn a lady in distress away from my door without offering some assistance. I didn't want her to have the impression that Alaska was a cold, unfeeling place."

"The fact that she was a young, beautiful woman had no bearing on your decision," Wade mocked with a taunting grin.

"She's engaged, too. Don't forget that," Noah inserted, drawing a laugh from the others, all except Wade Rafferty. A thoughtful frown creased his forehead, his gaze narrowing slightly.

"I haven't, dad," Cody said, and eyed Shannon with lazy intensity. "Although I admit there are times when I'd like to overlook that small detail."

"Do you have a photograph of your fiancé that I could borrow for a couple of days?" Wade asked. "I'll return it to you, of course."

"Yes, I have one." She opened her purse and rummaged through the contents for her billfold. Extracting Rick's picture from its clear plastic envelope, she handed it to Wade.

"Rick Farris—you said that was his name?" He studied the photo closely.

"Yes," she confirmed, and watched him with vague confusion. There was an undercurrent running through his attitude that she couldn't place.

Then he was smiling and the impression was gone. "I'll return it to you as soon as I can." He slipped the photograph into his wallet and turned to his wife, deftly changing the subject. "How about some coffee, Maggie?"

"Coffee and some streusel cake, fresh from the oven—your favorite, Cody," Maggie stated as she rose from the sofa.

"Sounds good, Maggie," he said with a nod.

"Would you like some help?" Shannon offered.

"No, I can manage. Thank you," Maggie refused.

A brief silence settled on the room after she'd left. Noah leaned forward in his chair, inserting himself in the conversation. "Has there been any word about your boss and his daughter?"

"No." Wade reached for a cigarette from the pack on the coffee table between the twin sofas. Lighting it, he studied the curl of gray smoke swirling into the air. "They've officially called off the air search, although any pilots flying in the area are keeping an eye out."

"What happened?" A faint frown lined Shannon's forehead as she divided her glance between the two men.

"We don't know," Wade replied. "The board chairman of my company and his daughter left for a long weekend to fly to a remote fishing camp. The plane never arrived at their destination. It's presumed it went down.''

"I'm sorry,'' she murmured awkwardly.

"Henderson was the pilot, wasn't he?'' Noah asked. When Wade confirmed that with a nod, he shook his grizzled head. "Damned good man. He knew more tricks than Houdini to keep a plane in the air. You can be sure it wasn't pilot error. I remember the time—''

"Don't go back in history, dad,'' Cody interrupted with a wry grimace. "Your memory is bound to falter.''

"My memory is as good as the day you were born,'' his father protested.

There was laughter in the glance he slid to Shannon. "Do you see what I mean? He's already wrong. I was born at midnight, not during the day.''

"Now, darn you, Cody! Quit twisting what I say,'' Noah declared in irritation.

"Are you two arguing already?'' Maggie appeared with a tray of refreshments. "I haven't been gone five minutes.''

The introduction of streusel cake and coffee brought a more congenial mood to the room's occupants. The conversation switched to other topics and the atmosphere became more relaxed as the shadows were banished to the far corners of the room.

Later, when Shannon offered to help clear away the dishes, Maggie accepted. "What's it like to live in Alaska?'' she asked as she followed the slim redhead into the kitchen.

"It's an adventure." The tone of Maggie's voice indicated that was an understatement. "Especially when you leave the city and go into the country. You certainly don't run to the corner store every other day. The isolation is harder on the women in the outlying communities than for those of us in Anchorage or Fairbanks. I don't suppose you've had much time to go sightseeing since you've arrived."

"No, I haven't," Shannon admitted.

"Because of his position, Wade spends a lot of time in Valdez. Be sure to pronounce it with a long *e* or the natives will quickly correct you," Maggie advised with a smiling glance. "Even with the pipeline terminal being located in Valdez, it's safe to say it isn't a bustling metropolis. Before Molly was born, I used to go with Wade on his trips to Valdez. It's still a very rural area; it has the necessities but few of the luxuries." She took the dishes from Shannon and stacked them in the sink. "It's an exciting region of the country, growing like a weed, its potential unrealized."

"Yes, Rick said the north was America's last frontier," she agreed.

"It's all that and more."

When they returned to the living room, the men were embroiled in a heavy conversation. Shannon caught Wade Rafferty's last statement, "I hope I'm wrong," before the discussion was abruptly halted by their approach. Cody's expression was troubled and grim, but it vanished the instant he met her look, to be replaced by a quick smile.

"Sorry we digressed into state politics," he said to explain the serious atmosphere.

"I certainly hope you settled all the issues," Maggie smiled.

"Naturally," Wade replied.

It was nearly an hour later when Cody made the suggestion they should leave. And it was another fifteen minutes before they actually made it to the door. Wade walked them to the car.

"I'll be in touch as soon as I have some definite answers," he promised.

Although the statement was more or less directed at Cody, Shannon thanked him. "I appreciate the time you're taking."

"My pleasure," he assured her, and waved as Cody reversed the car out of the driveway.

For a change, Noah Steele wasn't very talkative during the drive back to the hotel. Shannon was comfortable with the occasional silences that fell. The only subject discussed at any length was her impression of the Raffertys, which was a positive one.

Cody stopped next to the entrance to the parking lot first to let his father out. Before Noah climbed out, he started to ask, "Are you going to—"

"I'll be home directly, dad," Cody interrupted him.

"Okay." The older man stepped out and closed the rear passenger door.

Parking the car around the corner in front of the hotel, Cody got out to see Shannon safely to her room. Little was said during the ride up in the elevator or while walking down the hallway to her room. Shannon unlocked the door and turned to thank him for an enjoyable evening, but the probing search of his gaze distracted her.

"Is something wrong?" she frowned.

He leaned an arm against the door frame, a corner of his mouth lifting grimly. "Yes, something is wrong. Me. I'm wrong." Cody stated as his gaze possessively swept her upturned face to linger on her lips. "What I'm thinking is wrong." It slid lower to include the curved length of her body in a highly suggestive glance that lifted the tempo of her pulse. "What I'm wanting is wrong."

She was unnerved by his frankly sexual look, so blatantly demanding. "Cody, don't put me in a position where I'll have to refuse to see you again," she warned, to protect herself from the force of his maleness.

A nerve leaped along his jaw, exposing the raw edges of his desire, before the muscles relaxed and he smiled. "I won't. Do you believe in intuition, Texas, even when there aren't any facts to support it?"

The question puzzled her. Already on guard, she answered warily, "Sometimes ."

"So do I. And my intuition tells me that the time will come when what I'm thinking and what I'm wanting will be right—for both of us." He leaned down to brush her lips with a feather-warm kiss. "Good night, Texas." He pushed away from the door frame, leaving her free to enter the room. "I'm a patient man. All things come to he who waits."

Shannon stepped inside her room and closed the door, shaken by his absolute confidence. How could he be so supremely certain of her when she was engaged to Rick? It was absurd. But perhaps no more absurd than the ridiculous way her heart was thudding....

CHAPTER FIVE

THE NEXT MORNING Shannon was sitting beside the telephone debating whether she should call her parents and advise them of Rick's apparent disappearance. Saturday was approaching—her wedding day. She couldn't postpone the phone call much longer.

A knock at her door allowed Shannon to shelve the decision for the moment.

"Who is it?" she called.

"Cody!" was the partially muffled answer.

Unbolting the door, she slipped the night chain free and opened the door. "Good morning?" Her greeting held a question; she wondered what had brought him to the hotel at this hour.

"Good morning." He stood in the hallway with his hands thrust into the pockets of his flight jacket. A lazy smile slanted the strong line of his mouth. "I believe I owe you an apology for some of the things I said last night. I was out of line."

"It's forgotten." But she felt a twinge of regret that he hadn't meant them. Her attitude was really becoming confusing.

"Last night I guess I just wasn't looking forward to going home and sleeping alone in a double bed. An empty pillow gets to be pretty poor company. It's soft, but it doesn't generate any warmth," he explained with a shrug of his shoulders.

There was a tightening of her stomach muscles at this veiled discussion of a man and a woman sleeping together. She found it all too easy to visualize herself in his arms, shaped to his length spoon-fashion.

"Yes, I know," she agreed, but uneasily.

"I hope you don't have anything on your agenda this morning," Cody abruptly switched the subject. "I've decided that you've been cooped up in this hotel long enough. It's time you saw something of Alaska up close."

"But. . .don't you have to work?"

"That's one of the privileges of owning a business. You can take a day off whenever it suits you." When she continued to hesitate, Cody reasoned, "What would you do if you didn't go with me?"

"I . . . ." Her hand opened in an empty gesture.

"Nothing," he answered for her. "You need the break. Get your purse and a jacket."

It took her only a few seconds to collect both items and join him in the hallway. "Where are we going?" she asked as they entered the elevator.

"I thought we'd take a drive out to Matanuska Valley."

"I don't know any more than I did before," she laughed, because the name held no significance for her.

"You will," Cody promised.

In the car Cody took the highway that angled north from the city. The sky was predominantly blue, with gray white clouds lingering on the ridges of the Chugach Mountains. Homes began to thin out, the settlement giving way to an encroaching forest of trees dressed in the autumn colors of gold and rust. When they passed a highway sign that advised Moose Crossing—Next Ten Miles, Shannon turned to Cody with a disbelieving look.

"Moose crossing?" she repeated, certain it was a joke of some sort.

The corners of his mouth deepened in a half smile as he slid her a brief glance. "Except for some black-tailed deer on the islands, Alaska doesn't have any deer, but there are plenty of moose and caribou to make up for it. You'll see signs similar to that all along the highway. The moose like to browse on the young willow shoots that grow along the highway. Like the deer, you usually see them early in the morning or around sunset. A full-grown moose can weigh around a thousand pounds, so it isn't any joke if you run into one with a car."

"It certainly wouldn't be." The chance that she might catch a glimpse of one of the giants of the wild kept her gaze sweeping the undergrowth of the forests even though it was midmorning. The homes she saw scattered along the highway were more frequently constructed out of logs.

Miles slipped away as they traveled inland. The sight of a whole mountainside cloaked in shimmering gold leaves made her catch her breath in awe. It was a spectacle of nature in all its raw glory.

"What kind of trees are those? Aspens?" she questioned Cody, not believing she could be right.

"The gold ones? Yes."

Her head moved from side to side in awed disbelief. "I've been to the Colorado Rocky Mountains in the fall, where you often see a clump of golden aspen against a backdrop of pine. It's the other way around here. A clump of pine trees with a whole mountainside of aspens."

"Impressive, isn't it?"

"That's an understatement," Shannon declared on a fervent note, and turned to look at him. Her gaze was distracted by the glimpse of a plowed field beyond him. "Do they farm around here?" Farms did not fit her image of Alaska—so far nothing had matched her preconceived notion of Alaska.

"Matanuska Valley is the center of Alaska's agriculture," he verified.

"What do they grow?" Unconsciously she was still considering the climate too severe.

"Oats, wheat, barley, some vegetables." He

named off the crops, then added, "We'll stop at one of the produce markets near Palmer."

Her glance swept the valley to the left of the nighway. "I suppose they raise a lot of cattle."

"Not as much as you would expect. There isn't a high nutrient value in the native grasses. Most of the big cattle operations are located on Kodiak Island," he explained. "Matanuska Valley was settled during the Depression when much of the midwestern United States was stricken with drought. The Federal Government provided transportation for some two hundred families to come here and gave them land to develop and farm."

"I didn't know that." A brief look of chagrin spread across her features. "I'm beginning to realize there are a lot of things I don't know about Alaska. I should have been reading up on my history."

"Alaska has to be seen to be believed."

"I'm discovering that," Shannon agreed.

They drove through several small communities. The conversation between them subsided, leaving Shannon free to absorb the continually changing scenery that surrounded them. Mountains, valleys, wilderness, farms, log cabins, modern homes, rivers, lakes, ribbon-slim waterfalls splashing silver down the rock face of a mountain, marsh-wet lowlands—every curve in the road brought something new to see, sometimes at a better angle and sometimes just a tantalizing glimpse.

Outside of Palmer, Cody slowed the car and turned off the highway where a sign indicated the location of a farmers' market. Two cars were parked in front of a shed bearing a sign that read: Open. He stopped the car beside the other two and turned off the engine.

"Come on," he smiled. "We'll continue your education inside."

His remark aroused her curiosity as she climbed out and walked to the front of the car, where Cody waited for her. Together they walked to the shed's door, his hand resting lightly on the curve of her waist.

Astonishment registered in her expression within seconds after she stepped inside. She stared at the long tables with their picked-over selection of vegetables. Those that remained were so huge she doubted they were real. She walked over to a cabbage that weighed at least fifty pounds and touched a leaf.

"It's real," she murmured aloud, and lifted her rounded gaze to Cody. "How did it grow so big?"

"That isn't big," he denied as he critically studied the cabbage. "In fact, it's on the puny side."

"You're kidding!" Shannon breathed.

Cody gave her a look of mock surprise. "Don't cabbages grow this big in Texas?"

"You brought me here deliberately," she accused without anger, wising up to his game, "so you could brag about how big everything is in Alaska.''

"I don't have to brag, Texas. Alaska does it for herself.'' His smile was wide, laughter sparkling wickedly in his blue eyes.

She had to laugh, unable to dispute the accuracy of his remark. "You're going to have to explain to me how this cabbage grew so big,'' she insisted.

"It's very simple, really. Just a little bit of northern magic,'' Cody assured her. "This is the land of the midnight sun. The secret is almost twenty hours of sunlight during the day.''

"I hadn't thought about that. Does that much sunlight make everything grow like this?''

"It makes everything grow, but it doesn't always produce,'' he admitted. "Corn, for instance; the stalks and leaves are tall and healthy, but the ears are small and unformed.''

"Why?'' In the light of the way the sun affected other crops, she didn't understand why it didn't produce the same result with corn.

"You've heard the saying that at night you can hear the corn grow. In Alaska there is no night, only a kind of twilight. In order for corn to produce ears, you have to put it to bed— cover it the same way you cover a bird's cage, with cloth or a paper sack. Commercially, that isn't practical, although it's often done for family consumption in a home garden,'' he explained.

"That's amazing!" Shannon turned back to view the cabbage again, still marveling at its proportions. "Can't you imagine what a shock it was the first time someone planted a cabbage here and it grew into something like this? Talk about Jack and the Beanstalk!" she laughed, still finding it all a little incredible.

After they toured the small marketplace, they drove into Palmer and had lunch at the small café located inside the equally small hotel on the main street. Shannon was surprised at how hungry she was, cleaning up every bit of food on her plate. They returned to Anchorage at a leisurely pace, arriving back at her hotel in the early afternoon.

Suggesting coffee, Cody accompanied her into the hotel. "I think I'll check at the desk first, just to see if there are any messages for me," Shannon stated. As she started to cross the lobby, she recognized a couple standing in the center lobby.

"Cody, look! There's Wade and Maggie." When her glance swept back to him, she was surprised to find that he didn't appear pleased to see his friends. A thought occurred to her. "Do you suppose they found out something about Rick?"

"I don't know." He didn't venture an opinion as his hand applied pressure to the back of her waist, guiding her forward. "They've seen us. Let's go over and say hello."

So many times she'd had her hopes falsely

raised that she was almost afraid to hope Wade Rafferty had learned something about Rick's whereabouts. Crossing the lobby with Cody's hand firmly on her waist, she forced a smile to her lips and greeted the couple.

"Hello. We didn't expect to see you here this afternoon," she said, and glanced expectantly from one to the other, waiting for an explanation that would answer the looming question of what had brought them to the hotel.

Wade flicked a brief look at Cody, and Shannon felt his hand tighten its grip. When his enigmatic gaze returned to her, she was puzzled by its remoteness. "Last night when I told you your fiancé wasn't in the employ of our company, I was in error. His records were misplaced. I happened to show his photograph to a couple of our mechanics on the flight line; they recognized him as a pilot recently hired. They thought his name was Dick."

She had been bracing herself for another dead end. It was just beginning to hit her that she had finally found out where Rick was working. "I can't believe it!" she burst out on a happy note of relief. "Where is he? Where's Rick?"

"Steady, Texas," Cody's voice cautioned on an ominously low note.

"Cody's right," Wade stated briskly. "I'm afraid I don't have good news."

"What do you mean?" Alarm flashed across her face as Shannon suddenly became aware of the quiet sympathy and concern in Maggie's expression. "Is Rick all right? Has he been hurt?"

"He was flying copilot on the plane that carried Jackson Hale, our board chairman. There isn't any easy way to say this, Shannon." Wade's voice was heavy with regret. "The plane was reported missing more than two weeks ago, presumed lost with everyone aboard."

She stared. They were saying Rick's plane had crashed, implying that he was dead. It was in their faces. A tremor of disbelief started, gathering momentum.

"There must be a mistake," she murmured in vague protest. "Maybe it wasn't Rick."

Wade returned Rick's photograph, placing it in her nerveless fingers. "The ground crew identified him as the copilot. Henderson, our chief pilot, had hired him only the day before. We aren't certain whether the absence of any employment record was an oversight or if Henderson had it with his papers aboard the plane. Without it we weren't able to notify his next of kin. I'm sorry, Shannon. I'm truly sorry," he said grimly.

Her eyes blurred as she tried to look at the photograph in her hand. "No." It was a strangled sound of denial. She refused to accept that any of this was true.

"Come on." Cody's hand tightened around her waist, his voice brisk and commanding. "Let's go someplace less public than this lobby."

Shannon heard him, but she was barely conscious of being swept along to the elevators. Insulated by a numbed kind of shock, she kept hearing fragments of Wade's voice, phrases out of context: "presumed lost...flying copilot... next of kin...missing...sorry, sorry, sorry.. ."

"Where's the key to your room, Shannon?" Cody was asking, his voice coming from some far-off place. "Do you have your room key?"

His request penetrated her consciousness, but she lacked coordination as she fumbled with the flap of her shoulder bag. Cody slipped the strap off her shoulder and handed her purse to someone else, his arm remaining around her in silent support.

"See if you can find her room key, Maggie," he ordered.

She was absently aware of a door being opened. She was half walked and half carried into the room. Images danced in her mind of an airplane flying into a cloud and never coming out, swallowed by the vastness of the sky. She closed her eyes tightly, trying to shut out the vision.

"Wade, call down to room service and order up some black coffee with plenty of sugar," Cody ordered as he pushed her into a chair.

Her eyes opened to cling to his lean, strong-jawed face. There was the glitter of unshed tears in their hazel depths. A reluctant sadness was in his features, stamped with grimness.

"You weren't at all surprised when Wade told

me." Her voice was hoarse, but the haze was dissipating, clearing her head. "You knew...or guessed before he told me."

"Yes," Cody admitted.

"How long? How long have you known?" She felt betrayed by this man she had thought she could trust.

"I found out for certain only this afternoon, a few minutes ago, when I saw Wade in the lobby waiting for us. I *suspected* last night, after talking to Wade." He stressed the qualifying verb. "After talking to you, Wade realized that your fiancé could have been the unidentified copilot. That's why he wanted the photograph."

"You knew—you suspected, but you didn't tell me," Shannon accused. "I had a right to know."

"Maybe you did. But I didn't see the point of your losing a night's sleep when we weren't even certain Rick was on that plane," he retorted with a trace of anger. "I don't regret it and I'm not going to apologize."

"I won't thank you for it, either!" she flared.

"I never asked for your thanks," he countered with equal force. A heavy sigh broke from him as Cody lowered his head and rubbed the center of his forehead. "I'm sorry, Texas. I shouldn't have yelled at you." The anger of regret made his voice husky and rough. "I only wanted to make things a little easier."

There was a knock at the door and Wade

quietly announced, "Room service is here with the coffee."

Cody moved away to answer the door. Shannon watched his wide-shouldered frame with blurring eyes. A little late, she realized he had kept the suspicions from her in an effort to spare her additional anguish. Maggie knelt beside her chair and covered Shannon's clasped hands with her own.

"Cody was only thinking of you, Shannon," she murmured.

"I know." She bit at her lips, curving them in a rueful line. "I wasn't thinking."

"That's supposed to be my excuse," Maggie insisted, copying her rueful smile. "I'm always saying the first thing that comes to mind. Wade calls it being irritatingly frank." Her expression grew serious. "Will you be all right, Shannon? We have an extra bedroom. You are more than welcome to stay with us tonight."

"Thank you, but—" She was interrupted by Cody as he stopped beside her chair and offered her a cup of hot sweet coffee.

"Drink it." The determined set of his chin and the unyielding insistence of his gaze advised Shannon that he would physically help her if she refused.

"I know. It's supposed to be good for someone in shock," she murmured, and obediently sipped it. Even that small taste had a reviving effect, steeling her against the hopelessness that pressed on the edges of her mind. After the initial shock of Wade's news had eased, Shannon had already begun to fight back. The coffee just added strength.

"It there someone we could call?" Wade asked. "Anyone we should notify?"

"No." Shannon paused between sips of coffee. "I have to call my parents. They were going to fly here for the wedding on Saturday. They can contact Rick's uncle in Houston, the only relative he has."

"Come home with us," Maggie repeated her invitation. "I don't like the idea of your being here alone."

"Honestly, I'll be all right," she assured them. "There's no need for you to stay."

"Are you sure?" Wade persisted, eyeing her pallid complexion skeptically.

"Yes." She lowered her chin for a fraction of a second, then lifted it determinedly. "I know how busy you must be—how many other demands you have on your time. Thank you for coming over to tell me personally about... Rick."

Shannon refused to use any of their words like "lost" or "missing." She accepted the fact that the plane Rick had been flying hadn't reached its destination; she even accepted the possibility that it had crashed. But that didn't mean Rick was dead. People had survived air crashes before.

"If there is any way we can help, please call us." The sincerity in Maggie's green eyes left

Shannon in no doubt that it was not an idle offer.

"Thank you." A wan smile touched her mouth.

"I'll look after her," Cody stated, a proprietorial hand on her shoulder as he stood beside her chair.

"Let us know if there's anything we can do." Wade directed his statement to Cody while he and Maggie went through the motions of taking their leave. "There's some information the company will need, but we can get that later."

While Cody walked them to the door, Shannon remained in the armchair. Both hands were around the coffee cup. She lifted it to her mouth, draining the heavily sugared liquid. The three paused in the doorway, talking among themselves, but she wasn't interested in listening to their conversation. Pushing to her feet, she set the empty cup on a table and walked to the hotel window.

A mountain range thrust its ridge against the horizon. Her gaze scanned its rugged contours. Somewhere, far beyond those mountains, the plane had gone down—Rick's plane. She'd had a glimpse of the vastness of Alaska this morning—the Great Land, the brochures called it. Finding Rick in all that hugeness was going to be a monumental task, but she refused to consider that it was impossible. She hadn't come all this way just to catch the next plane home.

A pair of hands closed over her shoulders.

She knew they belonged to Cody even though she hadn't heard Wade and Maggie leave or the door close. She had felt the firm pressure of his touch often enough in the past few days to recognize it. The gentle kneading of her shoulders eased the raw tension in her nerves. She relaxed against the solid support of his tall frame, letting her head rest on the hard wall of his chest.

"What's out there, Cody?" There was a poignant softness to her question. "Beyond those mountains?"

"A valley, another range of mountains, a valley, mountains, and so on, and so on," he answered with a trace of grim acceptance.

Her breath caught in her throat at his answer, an affirmation of the huge expanse of land. The pressure of his hands turned her around, away from the window and into his arms. Their strength enfolded her in silent comfort. Shannon wound her arms around his middle, her cheek pressed against his chest. The solid beat of his heart was reassuring. She felt his mouth moving over her chestnut hair, the stirring warmth of his breath.

"This isn't the way I wanted it to turn out, Shannon." His voice was a low, gentle rumble. "Winning by default is not my idea of fair competition. I know it hurts, but it will fade in time. It always hurts to lose somebody you care about."

He was talking as if Rick were dead. Lifting

her head from his chest, she tipped it back to frown at him. "Just because the plane went down doesn't mean Rick was killed."

His hand lightly stroked her cheek, brushing a strand of hair behind her ear. It stayed to cup the side of her face while he bent his head to lower his mouth onto hers, warm and alive. Her lips clung to his a fraction of a second after the brief kiss ended, responding to the life force it conveyed.

"You have to be realistic, Shannon," Cody insisted quietly.

"I am. You don't know for certain that Rick is dead—that any of them are dead," she reasoned.

Patience stamped the expression on his strongly male features as he firmly reasoned with her. "The plane has been missing for more than two weeks. They haven't found a trace of the wreckage. There were no signal fires, nothing. If anyone survived the crash, it's doubtful he'd be alive now."

"Doubtful." She used his word to argue her case. "It's doubtful, but it's possible."

His mouth thinned in irritation. "You're twisting things to make them say what you want to hear. Don't do it. It's only going to make it harder." The hand around her waist continued to mold the lower half of her body against him, the muscled columns of his legs providing support.

"You can believe what you like, but he isn't

dead. I would know it if he were." Shannon refused to be swayed from her belief by any of his
arguments, no matter how valid they appeared
on the surface. "He's out there somewhere,
alive. I'll find him myself if I have to."

The anger of exasperation hardened his
features as Cody grew impatient with her.
"Don't be a stupid little fool. There are
thousands of acres of wilderness out there."

"Dr. Livingstone was found in the African
jungle," she reasoned.

"I suppose you think you are the Texas
equivalent of Stanley," he taunted acidly.
"You're crazy."

"I don't care," she flashed. "I won't give
up."

With an effort Cody gathered control of his
temper and tried once again to reason with her.
"I don't think you understand the number of
man-hours that have already been put in looking for that plane, how many aircraft took part
in the search. Jackson Hale wasn't an ordinary
fisherman. He was an important executive for a
very large firm. Cost was no object—not in
money, time, equipment, men, nothing!"

The glacial blue of his gaze was chilling.
Shannon recoiled from it, her hands pushing at
his waist. His grip shifted to her shoulders, his
fingers digging into the bones as Cody let her
step back but kept her in his reach.

"I don't care how hard anyone else has
looked," she declared.

"I suppose you plan to go out there by yourself and find him." His jaw was tightly clenched, ridging the muscles. "Would you mind telling me just how you propose to accomplish that?"

She faltered at his challenge, realizing she had been unconsciously counting on his support. "I wasn't exactly planning to do it alone...." Her hazel eyes made a silent appeal for his assistance.

His gaze narrowed on that look. "You don't expect *me* to go on this wild-goose chase with you? I have a business to run!"

"I wasn't going to ask you to do it for nothing." She was stung by his failure to offer his help. "I have some money saved." She didn't bother to explain that it was money set aside to buy things for the new home she'd planned to share with Rick. "I'll pay to charter your airplane."

"It isn't the money." He ground out the words angrily. "I don't want it."

"Then what is it?" Shannon demanded impatiently.

A low groan came from deep inside his throat. "Surely you've guessed by now, Texas." He hauled her roughly to him, bringing her within inches of his mouth. "Why should I help you find him when I want you for myself?"

No reply was permitted as he took possession of her lips, his arms encircling her to crush any resistance. The driving force of his kiss overpowered her senses, sweeping them under his domination. Boneless, weightless, she was a rag doll, compelled to submit to him.

Sheer possession didn't satisfy him. A subtle change began and spread. The hard anger of his mouth eased and attained a mobility. It began to urge, coax and demand more from her than limp acceptance. A response trembled inside her, hesitant and unsure. The supple caress of his hands nourished it along and it gained strength.

Dormant desires were aroused and made to burn through her flesh, awakening it to the delights of a man's touch, a man experienced in the ways to please a woman. She realized that as his nibbling mouth drew a moan from her throat.

"I can make you forget him." His huskily disturbed voice vibrated against the sensitive skin of her neck.

In a cold breath of sanity, Shannon discovered that he could. She was appalled by this weakness in herself. She twisted her head away from him.

"But I don't want to forget Rick," she insisted tightly, and strained to break the hold of his encircling arms. "If you won't help me find him, I'll hire someone else."

Cody had tasted her response. "Convince me that I should help you."

Earlier he had given her the reason. Shannon repeated it to him now. "Do you really want to win by default?"

His stillness was a visible thing, complete immobility for the space of a heartbeat. Then he was releasing her and pivoting away. Long, impatient strides carried him across the room to the door.

His name trembled on the tip of Shannon's tongue. She longed to call him back, to have the naked strength of his arms around her again and to feel the excitement of his kiss. She remained silent because she wasn't certain how much of her need was dictated by a dread of being alone.

She flinched as the door slammed with a barely restrained violence. She had counted on Cody's helping her. In such a short time she had come to depend on him. The sense of loss she felt was greater even than when Wade had informed her Rick had been aboard that missing plane.

CHAPTER SIX

THE TELEPHONE CALL to her parents was perhaps the most difficult one Shannon had ever made. Minus Cody's support, she nearly accepted her father's offer to fly to Anchorage to be with her. In the end she refused. Her mother attempted to persuade her to come home, but Shannon had already resolved to stay until she had exhausted every possibility of finding Rick.

Yet it was hard to know where to begin. She paced the hotel room, trying to decide on a plan of action and still hoping that Cody would relent and come to her aid. As the afternoon turned to dusk, then night, she began to accept that Cody felt under no obligation to help her.

A sudden knock on her door brought a rush of hope. She hurried to answer it, certain it would be Cody. But when she opened the door it was his father who was standing in the hallway. He craned his neck to peer beyond her into the room.

"Isn't Cody here?" he asked.

"No." She wasn't able to conceal her disappointment. "I haven't seen him since this afternoon. He left without saying where he was going or... *if* he'd be back."

A frown of concern added to the lines on his forehead as Noah Steele chewed his lower lip thoughtfully. "I haven't heard a word from him since this morning. That isn't like him. I talked to Wade." He paused, then glanced apologetically at Shannon. "I was sorry to hear about your fiancé. It's a terrible thing to find out after coming all this way."

"Rick isn't dead," she stated with absolute determination.

His eyes widened in surprise. "He isn't? But I thought Wade said—"

"It doesn't matter what Wade said," she interrupted, dismissing the conclusions reached by others. "Rick isn't dead. I would know if he were."

He studied her closely before answering. When he did, it was with a smile. "My mother always knew when there was something wrong and I was sick or in trouble. It was just some sixth sense she had that defied logic."

This was the first positive response she'd had. "Then you understand why I have to try to find him. I seem to be the only one who believes they're still alive."

"Sure, I understand," he nodded.

"Mr. Steele... Noah," she corrected, "will you help me?" She saw his hesitation and guessed the reason for it. "I've already asked

Cody. I even offered to pay him, but he refused me."

"He refused? I would have been ashamed of him if he'd taken money for helping you." He looked indignant and puzzled. "But why did he refuse to help?"

"He thought it was a wild-goose chase." Which was partly the truth.

"Maybe it is, but he should have kept his opinion to himself and helped you anyway. Believe me, I'll give him a piece of my mind the next time I see him," he promised in a threatening manner.

"Will you help me, Noah? I don't know where to start," Shannon admitted.

"Of course I will," he assured her.

"Good." She sighed in relief. "Come in so we can decide what to do first."

Pushing the door open wider to admit him, she pivoted to return to the center of the hotel room. After a second's hesitation he followed her inside, but left the door standing ajar, as dictated by the sense of propriety that frowned on a man's being in a single woman's room with the door closed.

"The first thing we need to do is check with the flight service and get a copy of the flight plan they filed," Noah began.

"Never mind, dad." Cody's voice inserted itself in the conversation. Shannon whirled around to see him framed in the open doorway. There was a hard-bitten set to his features and a wintry-blue frost to his gaze. "I've already done that."

"Cody?" His father recovered first. "What are you doing here? We weren't expecting you."

Brisk strides carried him into the room—very emotionless, very professional. "I also have copies of the search grids, weather reports from both the pilots in the vicinity and the bureau on the day the plane disappeared, and any other data that might be helpful."

He stopped short of Shannon, his feet slightly spread apart in a challenging stance. "Have you...changed your mind?" The answer seemed fairly obvious, yet she had to ask.

"Shannon told me that you weren't going to help her," Noah explained in some confusion.

"I'm going to help her." A crack appeared in the emotionless mask that had hardened on his features. Shannon caught a glimmer of that warm sparkle she usually saw in his eyes. His mouth quirked along a familiar line. "I've never been second best in my life. You might as well know that I'm used to coming in first."

Her smile was slow in forming. "I guessed that." His message was loud and clear. He still wanted her for himself. He would help her find Rick, but he was equally determined that after he did, he was going to win out over Rick.

Once she would have said that was impossible. She had believed the six months' separation from Rick would ultimately strengthen their marriage. After knowing Cody these few short days, she had doubts—small ones, little questions, vague uncertainties. Her faith in the emotion she felt for Rick was just a little shaken.

But none of those doubts stopped her from being glad that Cody had come back. As long as he was there, she had the feeling everything was going to be all right. She couldn't explain it— any more than she could explain why she was so certain Rick was alive.

"When do we start?" she asked.

"Tomorrow. I'll be by to pick you up at seven in the morning," Cody answered. "Bring along what clothes you'll need for two or three days, but pack light. The hotel will store your excess luggage. Do you have a winter coat, a heavy parka, something warm?"

"Yes, I have a parka, long underwear, the works." Her smile broadened to show the dimples in her cheeks. "My mother insisted I bring it all along. I think she was under the impression that Alaska never thawed out."

"Bring the parka; you might need that. But the long underwear can stay in mothballs for a couple more weeks." The amused edges of his mouth deepened with shared humor.

"Where are you going?" his father wanted to know.

"We're going to refly the route listed on their flight plan, and improvise after that."

"In that case, I'm going with you," Noah stated.

"Dad." Cody's voice was heavy with patient

reasoning as he turned his head to eye his father. "One of us has to stay here to keep the business going. We can't both be gone."

"You said yourself that it would be only a couple of days. Sy Turner can look after things. It can't be much of a business if it falls apart when the two of us are gone for a few days," he challenged. "Besides, Shannon asked if I'd help her look for her fiancé, and I said I would. I can't go back on my word."

"I did ask him," she admitted when Cody's glance slid to her. "You walked out and I...." She shrugged vaguely. "I didn't think you were coming back."

His gaze moved to linger on her mouth and vividly remind her of the driving possession of his kiss, so sensually demanding yet persuasive. That odd tremor started again, reminding her that he was capable of disturbing her much more deeply than she had imagined.

"You should have known better," was all the comment he made.

His astute father was conscious of the subtle undercurrents that charged their innocent exchange, eyeing them both. "Even if Shannon hadn't specifically asked me, I'd be going along anyway," he stated. "A young single woman shouldn't go gallivanting off into the wilds with a bachelor for two or three days unless she has an older person along."

"You could be right, dad." Cody's agreement caught Noah off balance. He had expected more of an argument from his son.

"You can argue all you like, Cody, but I'm coming with you," he replied automatically.

Cody was patient, smiling. "Dad, I agreed that you should come."

"You did?" He faltered an instant, then recovered. "That's sensible of you."

Even though she kept silent during the brief discussion, Shannon concurred. She accepted the wisdom of having Noah along as a kind of chaperon. That passionate kiss had altered the relationship between her and Cody. Once communication had been established on an intimate level they could never retreat from it. The knowledge of it would always be there, running through their glances, their words, the most innocent touch. They needed the presence of a third person to act as a buffer. Shannon knew it and so did Cody.

The weight of his glance was on her, reading her thoughts but passing no comment. "Can you be ready by seven in the morning?" he asked instead.

"Yes." Somehow, although it meant a lot of packing and sorting and organizing all the loose ends.

"Dad will pick you up at the main entrance. Wear slacks, something comfortable and warm," Cody advised.

"Yes." It was an all-encompassing agreement to his suggestions.

"Ready, dad?" Cody questioned. "We have a lot of things to do, too, before tomorrow morning."

"Right," he nodded with a show of authority, then had to hurry to catch up with Cody, who was already walking to the door. "See you in the morning."

"Yes." Shannon followed to close the door after them. "Good night," she said to both of them.

From Cody she received a slanting smile of acknowledgment while his father responded, "Good night—and be sure to lock the door."

"I will," she promised.

Once they were out of sight in the hallway, she closed the door and slipped the bolt and night chain in place. For an instant she paused, realizing that the eagerness she felt within had nothing to do with finding Rick. It sobered her to the task at hand.

As ORDERED, Shannon had packed light, taking only the essentials she'd need for three days and storing the rest of her things at the hotel. Dressed in fur-lined boots, a pair of forest-green corduroy jeans and a bulky cream-colored sweater, she was ready and waiting precisely at seven o'clock the next morning in the hotel lobby.

Noah Steele picked her up. "Cody is waiting for us at the plane, getting it all checked out so we can leave as soon as we get there."

They had traveled several blocks before she realized it wasn't the route to Merrill Field. "Aren't we going the wrong way to the airport?" she asked hesitantly.

"We aren't going to the airport, leastwise not that airport," Noah replied. "We're going to use the floatplane."

"Oh." Her concern subsided as she settled back in the passenger seat and looked out the window at the scattered clouds in the sky.

As though bothered by her silence, Noah stole several glances at her. "The weather forecast says it will be clear by midmorning, so we should have good weather," he told her, then appeared to decide she needed further assurance, because he began to lecture her about flying. "With your fiancé's plane being missing and all, it's natural for you to be a little nervous about going up. Here in Alaska we average a light plane crash practically every day of the year. Those are kinda scary statistics."

"The number is higher in Texas." She had learned a lot of facts about flying from Rick, so she also knew that the population of Texas was considerably more than Alaska's which meant the risk was higher here.

"What those stastics don't tell you," Noah continued, not paying any attention to her comment, "is about the pilot flying the plane. Bush pilots have got quite a reputation. It sounds romantic and exciting to these young kids. Before the ink is dry on their pilot's licenses, they're up here to become bush pilots. Just like your Rick. They don't know the weather, the terrain or their plane, and they wind up taking foolish chances with all three. But they aren't the only ones."

Pausing, he glanced over to see if she was listening. She was, mostly because she was confused. She thought he had intended to assure her how safe it was to fly, but he seemed to be trying to shake her confidence.

"There aren't many *old*, experienced bush pilots." He stressed the adjective. "Even if they're born and raised here, somewhere along the line they find themselves in a situation where they feel they have to live up to their reputation of getting through no matter what. They take off when the weather's bad or won't turn back when they hit a storm front, or keep going even when they're low on gas. They'd rather crash than have someone question their manhood by doubting their bravery."

"That's stupid and dangerous," Shannon responded with a frown.

"Yep," he nodded. "But Cody ain't like that. He's the best damned bush pilot flying today. He knows it and he doesn't feel that he has to prove it. So you don't have to worry about flying with him. You're as safe as if you were in your momma's arms."

So that was what all this had been leading up to. Shannon smiled to herself. The message was loud and clear: he was assuring her of the com-

petency of their pilot, because pilots crashed
planes. Only rarely was it the other way around.

"Thank you, Noah. I do feel better," she
said, and he appeared satisfied that he had succeeded in his self-appointed task.

When they arrived at the lake, one of several
in the Anchorage area, the plane was fueled and
preflighted, ready to go. All the gear was
aboard with the exception of the suitcase Shannon had brought. Noah passed it to Cody so it
could be stowed in the luggage compartment.

"Do you want to ride in the front seat,
Texas?" Cody asked.

"Sure."

It was a peculiar sensation to climb into a
plane that was bobbing on the water like a boat.
It was a single-engine craft with aerodynamical-
ly designed floats instead of landing gear. Shannon buckled herself into the right seat while
Noah settled himself in the seat behind her.

Climbing into the pilot's seat, Cody buckled
his seatbelt and went through the final checklist.
The engine throbbed with power, overcoming
the drag of the water. The floatplane was a new
experience for Shannon. As he taxied away
from the shore and turned the plane into the
wind, Cody steadily opened the throttle to full
power. The sensation of moving over water
gradually decreased until the aircraft was
smoothly skimming the surface and lifting off in
a steady climb.

Takeoffs always gave Shannon a little rush of

exhilaration. No longer earthbound, she was flying free. She glanced at Cody to see if he shared the sensation, the glitter of excitement in her brown eyes.

The smoke-colored lenses of his sunglasses shaded his eyes but didn't hide them. Shannon could see him meet her glance. A brief smile curved his mouth as if in response before he returned his attention to the business of flying. The sunglasses were not an affectation but a necessary protection, shielding his eyes from the glare of the sun, which could blind him to other aircraft in the vicinity.

She was discovering how many little pieces of information she had picked up from Rick, small things that allowed her to recognize the competence of this pilot. Surreptitiously she studied the man behind the metal-framed sunglasses, the chiseled strength in his profile and the sheen of rumpled velvet in his hair, which was black as pitch. He was calm, and alert, with an air of proficiency. Shannon was conscious of feeling absolutely secure with Cody at the controls. It was a powerful feeling, strong and pulsing through her.

His moving glance encountered her gaze, made a brief scan of her face and swung back to the front. "I have activated our flight plan," Cody said, referring to the radio communication he had just completed. "They made a stop in Valdez, so we will, too. We can stretch our legs and grab a cup of coffee."

Shannon nodded her agreement with the suggestion. They headed east where the Chugach Mountains stood. The city of Anchorage spilled onto their sides, pinning houses on their slopes. But civilization was left quickly behind and Shannon was caught by the vastness that was Alaska. It was the green and gold of white spruce and aspen, the blue of the sky and sparkling water; it was wild and raw, majestic and limitless.

As the plane crossed the neck of Kenai Peninsula, the island-dotted waters of Prince William Sound glittered in the morning sunlight. The Gulf of Alaska lay beyond. There was a predominance of white on the mountains that crowded the sound. This was the snow Shannon had expected to see in Alaska.

"Snow." She pointed it out to Cody.

He glanced at her and shook his head. "You're half-right."

Then Noah leaned forward, sticking his head between the seats. "Why don't you fly by the Columbia so Shanon can see it?"

"I planned on it," Cody answered, then explained to Shannon what they were talking about. "We're coming up on the Columbia Glacier. It's literally a river of solid ice, all four hundred fifty-odd square miles of it. That's an area almost the size of Los Angeles."

Through the smoke-gray lenses of his sunglasses, Shannon saw the roguish gleam in his

light-colored eyes. "But you're not bragging,"
she inserted with a knowing smile.

The corners of his mouth deepened attractive-
ly with the shared humor of their private joke.
Pleasure sent its roots deep within her and
lightened her spirits. After last night she wasn't
able to regard their relationship as strictly
platonic. She had been aroused by Cody's ad-
vances, more so than was comfortable for her
peace of mind. And she had become concerned
that they might not be able to reestablish an easy
communication marked by intimate sparring.
But the bond between them hadn't been damaged, and she was glad.

As they approached the glacial formation,
Shannon was able to see the course of the giant
white ribbon of ice, pushing its way through the
mountain forests toward the sea. When they
reached its point of terminus, her breath ran
from her.

"It's so blue." She turned to Cody in surprise, because the sheer-faced glacier had a
definite sky-blue coast rising hundreds of feet
up from the water.

"It looks even more blue on a cloudy day.
The ice is like a prism, refracting the light," he
explained, and banked the plane so that she
could have a better look. "Do you notice the
color of the water?"

It was a dirty gray, littered with huge chunks
of ice that had broken off the glacier. The ice
chunks seemed unimpressive until she noticed

an excursion boat weaving its way through them and realized that many of them were full-fledged icebergs.

"The water is referred to as glacier milk because of the silt, debris and powdered rock it carries." He made a steeper bank and pointed. "We have some harbor seals down there, sunning on the ice."

"I see them," Shannon confirmed, spying the dark specks on the ice floes.

"Quite often there are whales in the area, but I don't see any this morning," Cody said. "I can make a three-sixty if you want to see more of the glacier."

Shannon hesitated for only an instant. No matter how fascinated she was by the massive river of ice, this wasn't a sight-seeing expedition. "No, let's go on to Valdez," she replied.

"We're on our way." He smoothly leveled the plane and resumed his original course and speed.

Leaving the glacier area behind, they flew on. This bird's-eye view of the country from the aircraft window began to widen Shannon's perspective of the situation. She hadn't appreciated what Cody meant when he tried to warn her that finding the wreckage of Rick's plane was like looking for a needle in a haystack. There were hundreds of miles of emptiness out there, and a gnawing sense of futility grew inside her. She silently struggled with it as she gazed out the window at the awesome reaches of wilderness.

"The Valdez Narrows are just ahead." Cody nodded to the front. "The authorities allow only one oil tanker to pass through the straits at a time. It's always accompanied by two tugs just in case it loses steerage. Only two tankers are permitted in the port itself at any one time."

He had begun his descent, and the nose-down attitude of the plane gave Shannon a clear view of the narrow passage of water leading into the harbor. Mountain slopes formed the walls of the strait, less than a mile wide. Shannon waited expectantly for her first glimpse of the bustling port city of Valdez.

Mountains formed a chain around the harbor, a dramatic setting with rugged peaks in the foreground in every direction. The huge oil-storage tanks were clustered along the southern side of the harbor behind a containment dike, as well as the many buildings housing the offices and shops of the operations center. But Shannon could see nothing of a city except for a small town on the north side of the harbor.

"Where is Valdez?" she asked.

"That's it on the left." He reached down to adjust the trim of the aircraft.

"That?" She frowned in skepticism when he indicated the small town.

"Yeah. Why? Is something wrong?" Cody allowed his glance to touch her once, busy with his landing preparations.

Her shrug was uncertain. "I thought it would be much bigger. Since it's the terminal for the

Alaska pipeline. I guess I was expecting to see Houston, Texas."

Cody smiled his understanding. "Check your seat belt," he advised as they started their landing approach to the harbor.

Once they were on the water and taxiing toward shore, Noah leaned forward again. "The tidal wave that followed the Good Friday earthquake in 1964 destroyed or damaged practically every building in Valdez. What you see here isn't the original townsite. They moved the town four miles to this location and rebuilt it. The location was chosen for the terminus of the pipeline because this harbor is one of the northernmost ice-free ports in this hemisphere."

"What happened to the old townsite?"

"They leveled it off. There's nothing left of it now," Noah explained, and settled back into his seat.

Their stop in Valdez was brief. They stayed long enough to stretch their legs, have some coffee and refuel the aircraft. Then they were taking off again, this time heading north across the alpine summits of the Chugach Mountains. They flew over Keystone Canyon with its spectacular rock formations and crystal-bright waterfalls.

Shortly afterward Shannon had her first glimpse of the pipeline. From the air it was a silver thread bumping over hillocks and running straight on flatter land, then disappearing underground to reappear farther along. There was an endless variety of things to see—more glacial areas, spruce forests, tundralike meadows above the tree line. Lakes were sprinkled around the terrain like fat raindrops. Everywhere there seemed to be the sparkle of water. As they flew over a lake in a very sylvanlike setting, Shannon couldn't help remarking on its untouched beauty.

"One of the states in the lower forty-eight is known as the land of ten thousand lakes," Cody remarked.

"Yes, that's Minnesota," Shannon inserted.

"I thought you should know that Alaska doesn't have ten thousand lakes." Cody paused deliberately. "At the last count, we had more than three million, in round figures. Mind you, I'm not bragging."

"No, of course not," she laughed.

As her gaze swung to the front again, she noticed what appeared to be a massive white cloud bank looming on the horizon. "Look. Is that a storm front?"

"That, Texas, is the Wrangell Mountains," Cody informed her. "A range unparalleled in sheer magnificence and grandeur."

She looked closer and realized that the clouds were really lofty, snow-covered peaks towering above the landscape. In awed silence she watched them take shape and form—rugged and wild and breathtaking.

CHAPTER SEVEN

THE GLACIER-CLAD MOUNTAINS were a wilderness of forests, lakes and rivers. They were all she could see in any direction, and the plane had penetrated only the outer edge of the massive range, which encompassed an area of some six thousand square miles. Fifty miles back, Cody had informed her that they were passing the last known spot where there had been confirmed contact with Rick's plane. It had gone down somewhere out here. But where? Her eyes strained in their search of the rugged terrain below.

From the rear passenger seat, Noah spoke up. "Is something wrong, son?"

The quick, serious tone of the man's question swung Shannon's attention to the cockpit of the private plane. Cody's expression was cool and steady, but she sensed a heightened alertness. His attention never left the instrument panel as he replied to his father in a calm, very matter-of-fact voice.

"We're losing oil pressure. I'm going to set her down in that lake over there." He indicated the body of water a mile to their left, then cast a look at Shannon and smiled in quiet assurance.

"Don't worry. This is just a precaution. We may not even have a problem."

She nodded her understanding and tried to ignore the twinges of uneasiness. There was no change in the rhythmic power of the engine, which supported Cody's implied assertion that the plane's performance had not been affected—at least, not yet. She listened while he radioed their approximate position and an advisory of their situation. When his transmission was acknowledged, he sideslipped the plane to achieve a rapid and controlled loss of altitude.

It wasn't an emergency situation, and Cody was landing to make certain it didn't become one. Somebody knew where they were and why. Shannon kept thinking that it hadn't been that way for Rick. Whatever had gone wrong, either there hadn't been time for a distress call or else it had never been received.

They landed smoothly and without incident. "I noticed a log cabin tucked back in the woods," Noah said when Cody adjusted the throttle to taxi. "It was over on the north side just as we were setting down."

Following the directions of his father, Cody taxied the plane back to the general area Noah had described. Shannon spied the cabin he had seen when they were landing and pointed it out to Cody. He taxied the plane to the very edge of the graveled shoreline.

"It looks like it's deserted," Noah observed as the engine was switched off. "If anybody were living there, he'd be out here to find out what we wanted."

The primitive cabin built of logs was small, roughly ten foot square. Nothing stirred as they climbed out of the plane. There was a cache near the cabin, elevated high off the ground on legs and accessible by a homemade ladder. "We might as well take a look around," Cody said when the aircraft was secure.

"It's probably all shut up." It seemed reasonable to Shannon, since it had obviously been abandoned.

"If it is, it wasn't an Alaskan who owned it," Noah stated. "It's custom to leave a cabin open and stocked for anyone in need who might come along."

The wooden door had swelled, but it opened at the urging of Cody's shoulder. The owner of the cabin had observed the Alaskan custom. The single-room structure had an earthen floor and a low ceiling. Firewood was stacked in a corner along with shavings for kindling. In addition to a barrel stove, there was a crudely made table and chair and a bunk bed. Matches were in a waterproof container on the table along with sacks of flour, powdered milk and sugar. A kerosene lamp was full and equipped with a new wick.

"There are probably dried beef and vegetables in the cache, as well," Cody surmised. "At least if we're stuck here for long we won't starve." He turned toward the door and clamped a hand on his father's shoulder. "Come on, dad. Let's go see what is causing that pressure drop."

"Can I help?" Shannon asked.

"For the time being you might as well relax and enjoy the scenery," Cody advised.

Shannon followed them back to the plane, partially beached on the lakeshore, and watched them work on it for a while. Eventually she tired of that. The lakeshore beckoned her to explore it, so she began to stroll along its edge, not intending to wander out of sight of the plane.

The air smelled incredibly fresh and pure, tangy with the scent of pines. Birches and willows grew abundantly along the lake. The distinctive mound of a beaver dam led her on to take a closer look. On a fallen timber she took up watch and was rewarded with the sight of a large beaver swimming toward its home after a half hour's wait.

By sheer chance she sighted a giant moose grazing on the opposite side of the lake. Even at that distance she could tell that the spread of his antlered rack was wider than she could stretch both arms. She considered returning to the cabin's clearing, then curiosity changed her mind and she walked a little farther to see what was beyond the next bend in the lake.

Before she had gone three feet, she thought she heard someone shouting. She stopped to listen. "Shannon!" It was Cody. The imperative summons of his voice turned her around.

"I'm coming!" she shouted in answer, and hurried to retrace her route.

But she had gone farther than she'd realized, and she was out of breath by the time she spotted the plane. She slowed down to catch her wind. A ruefully apologetic expression swept over her face when she saw Cody striding toward her.

"Don't you know better than to wander off like that?" He sounded impatient and angry.

"Sorry," she said breathlessly. "I didn't realize I had gone so far." Then she noticed the revolver in his hand. Her winded laugh was confused. "What were you going to do? Find me and bring me back at gunpoint?"

"This is bear country, Texas." He tucked the revolver inside his waistband. "You could have met up with some 'griz' for all I knew."

"You mean a grizzly bear?" she repeated with a trace of apprehension. "You don't really believe there are any close by, do you?"

"I don't know how close one might be right now," Cody admitted, and waved a hand at a tree several feet from where she was standing. "But I do know the claw marks on that tree aren't more than a couple of days old." As she turned to look at the white scratches on the tree's trunk, scratches higher than her head, he explained, "That's the way they mark their territory. So don't go wandering off anymore."

"I won't." It was a fervent promise, his implied warning not one that needed to be repeated. She glanced at the plane and saw Noah working on the engine. "Isn't the plane fixed?"

"No, but we think we've located the problem."

"Can it be fixed?" Here they were, out in the middle of nowhere, and Shannon didn't want to think about the possibility that it couldn't be repaired.

"Dad can jerry-rig anything, but it might take a while," Cody replied with a confident patience. "That's why I was looking for you. I thought I'd see if you wanted to take a stab at lighting that stove and fixing us something to eat."

"I'll give it a try," she agreed.

"Check the cache, but be careful of the ladder," he cautioned.

The cache held a treasure trove of articles. Besides rice, beans, powdered eggs, dried vegetables and beef, Shannon found sleeping bags, long johns, mukluks, mittens and candles. There wasn't any coffee, but she did find a can of tea.

Lighting the wood-burning barrel stove turned out to be a case of trial and error. Then she had to haul water from the lake and wait for it to boil on the stove top in order to wash the frying pans and dishes she found.

It was well into the afternoon before she had a meal on the table. It wouldn't have won any cooking prizes, but under the circumstances everyone agreed it was satisfactory. When they had finished, they took their tea outside to drink it. Somehow the fresh air added to its strong flavor.

"We aren't going to get the plane fixed much

before nightfall," Cody stated. "I'm not that familiar with this area to feel comfortable flying at night, so you might as well plan on spending the night here."

"In other words, start cooking supper now so it will be ready by dark." Shannon mocked the length of time it had taken her to fix a lunch in these primitive conditions.

"Something like that," Cody agreed with a taunting grin.

"Aren't you glad I came along?" Noah demanded. "Now you have someone who not only can fix your plane but also can be a chaperon tonight to keep everything respectable."

"Dad—" Cody eyed him with bemused affection "—I don't think you want me to answer that question." His gaze traveled over Shannon in a deliberately suggestive manner, blatantly teasing as opposed to blatantly sexy—although there was a subtle hint of that, too.

"I have never seen a laughing leer in my life," Shannon declared.

"Stick around, Texas." The expression in his eyes changed, heavy with meaning. She felt the tripping of her pulse. "There are a lot more things I'd like to show you sometime—when dad isn't around."

She tried to make light of his remark. "You're just a sore loser."

"Wouldn't you be?" he countered. "Tonight we are going to sleep in the same room. . .with pop."

Noah frowned in gruff disapproval. "Cody, you shouldn't be talking like that to her. It's her fiancé we're out here to find."

"Right," Cody agreed thoughtfully. "I guess that slipped my mind."

"You just remember that," Noah stated with an insistent nod.

There was a responding quirk of his mouth, but no reply. Shannon fully understood that Cody planned to pursue her in his own way regardless of the ring on her finger. Recognizing that, she also recognized that she was finding a disturbing thrill in the chase. As she noticed how closely he was watching her, she wondered if he could see that. Then she saw the gleam of satisfaction in the light blue depths, and knew he had.

Draining the last of his tea from the metal cup, Cody handed it to her, then turned to his father. "Let's get back to work."

As the two men walked to the plane, Shannon carried the cups into the cabin and began the task of cleaning the dishes. She had started the evening meal when she heard the drone of an approaching airplane. It was an alien sound in this wilderness. Frowning, she walked to the door of the cabin and watched as it swooped low to circle the cabin.

Cody signaled something to the plane. The message was acknowledged with a wag of its wings before it flew off.

"What did he want?" Shannon called.

"He was checking to see if we needed any assistance," Cody replied. "I signaled that we had everything under control."

"Do you?"

"Yeah, if we can figure out how to put it back together," he grinned.

She was smiling as she reentered the cabin. Cody had an irresistible sense of humor to go with his reckless smile and bold eyes, but what made him so formidable was his swift, keen intelligence. And it was all wrapped up in a handsome package. Absently she fingered her engagement ring, conscious only of a vague discontent. She shrugged the feeling away and went back to her work.

Either Shannon discovered the knack of cooking on the wood stove or else luck was on her side, because dinner turned out near perfect. The skillet biscuits were a little too brown on the bottom, but the vegetable-beef stew was delicious. So was the rice pudding with dried raisins.

By the light of the kerosene lamp, she washed the dishes while Cody dried them. Noah went to great lengths to ensure both were aware of his presence in the cabin. It didn't seem to matter. The steadiness of Cody's bold look didn't need any words to get his message across and succeeded with unnerving ease.

When the dishes were finished and everything was put back where they'd found it, Cody suggested, "Let's go outside and sit on the porch. It's a beautiful night."

Shannon had already noticed the brilliance of the stars in the sky outside the window. The call of the quiet Alaskan night beckoned to her. She was tempted to agree, but the temptation was more than the beauty of the night. Looking at Cody, she knew what else was tempting her. For that reason she refused.

"No, thanks." She tried to sound very casual about it. "It's been a long day and I'm kind of tired."

"You're right." Noah was quick to agree with her decision. "We should all have an early night. Morning's gonna be here before we know it."

"Absolutely." Cody's dry voice seemed to mock both of them.

"You can sleep in that bunk bed, Shannon," Noah instructed with a gesturing wave of his hand. "Cody and I will sack out on the floor."

"Okay," Shannon nodded.

"Are you sure your old bones can take sleeping on the floor, dad?" Cody challenged, a wicked glint dancing in his eyes. "Maybe you should take the bunk and let me and Texas have the floor."

"Don't you go worrying about my bones." Noah quickly rejected the idea, but not before Shannon's heart had done a little somersault at the implication behind Cody's words.

If they had both slept on the floor, he would have arranged it so that they weren't sleeping apart. Yet he had known his father would never go along with the suggestion. It had been a clever ploy to keep her awareness of him aroused. Just for a minute, her imagination ran away with itself as she pictured what it would be like to sleep curled against his vital male form. She made the mistake of looking at him and saw his look darken vibrantly when he read in her eyes what she was thinking. She turned away.

"Now you've gone and done it," Noah accused his son. "You've embarrassed her with your sly hints about sleeping together."

"Did I *embarrass* you, Texas?" The slight stress he put on the verb indicated that he knew embarrassment wasn't her reaction.

"No." Shannon mocked him with an over-the-shoulder glance letting him see that she knew his game, too. "And I don't think that's what you were trying to do, either, was it?"

Cody arched a glance at his father. "I think she's getting wise to me, dad."

"It's about time." Noah showed his impatience with his son's behavior. "Cody and I will step outside while you get yourself ready for bed," Noah told her. "You just give us a shout when it's all right to come in."

"Or if you need any help," Cody inserted with his customary bold look.

"I'm sure I can manage without any help," Shannon replied dryly.

"Pity," he murmured with mock regret. "I'm good at buttons and zippers." Then he winked broadly, making it all something to laugh about.

While his father ushered him out the door with a show of irritation, Shannon silently shook her head at Cody's irresistible brand of charm. It was simply impossible to be offended by anything he said, not when humor glinted so readily in his eyes.

Opening the suitcase Noah had brought up from the plane earlier that evening, she took out the few things she would need that night. The long-sleeved flannel nightgown reached down to the floor and buttoned all the way to the neck. It was just about as modest and unsexy as a nightgown could get. Shannon smiled when she considered Cody's probable reaction to it.

Leaving her socks on so her feet would be certain to stay warm, she climbed inside the sleeping bag spread over the bunk. She lay there for a few minutes, listening to the low murmur of voices coming from the outside.

"Okay!" she called finally. "You can come in now!"

Only one set of footsteps crossed the wood floor of the porch to the door. Shannon recognized the shuffling tred as Noah's. A little frown of disappointment creased her forehead as the door opened and Noah entered alone. He paused before closing the door and looked outside.

"Don't stay out too late, Cody," he addressed his unseen son with paternal concern. "You need your rest the same as we do."

"I won't," came the promise, and Shannon

heard the dry affection and amusement in Cody's voice. "Good night, dad." Then louder, "Good night, Texas. Sweet dreams."

"Good night," she called back, and snuggled a little deeper into the sleeping bag.

Her mouth curved slightly from an inner contentment she couldn't define. After Noah had settled into his sleeping bag on the floor, Shannon listened to the gentle night sounds for a while. She closed her eyes, not expecting to fall asleep until after Cody had turned in for the night. Yet at some point she drifted off.

A persistent hand nudged her shoulder to awaken her. She stirred, frowning a sleepy protest, and turned her head to this inconsiderate person disturbing her sleep. In the darkness of the cabin, all she could make out was a black form bent close to the cot.

"What...?" Her sleep-husky voice attempted to demand the reason for being wakened in the middle of the night.

But she was promptly requested to keep still. "Sshsh." Her tiredness was chased away by the sound of Cody's voice when he whispered, "Put your coat on and come outside. There's something I want to show you."

Without giving her a chance to refuse or disagree, his dark shape stole away from the cot and glided silently to the door. She sat up as he slipped outside. Despite all the arguments that could be made as to why she shouldn't go, her curiosity was aroused.

Taking care not to make any noise that might wake Noah, Shannon crawled out of the cot. It wasn't easy trying to find her things in the dark. She had to move slowly and cautiously. With her shoes on and her coat over the flannel nightgown, she tiptoed to the door and stepped onto the porch.

It was lighter outside than she'd expected. She easily saw Cody standing a few feet from the cabin. A quick glance around the area didn't find anything of interest. Cody turned as she hesitated by the door.

"Come here." He motioned her to his side, his voice still pitched low.

Uncertainly she moved to him. "What is it?"

His gleaming blue eyes held her gaze for a long moment, setting off alarm bells of warning. "At night the stars are supposed to be big and bright, deep in the heart of Texas. I wanted to show you the magic of an Alaskan night."

As she looked into his eyes, all sorts of magic seemed to be happening inside her. A sensible part of her knew that wasn't what he meant. With difficulty she directed her gaze away from him toward the night sky and found the source of light brightening the darkness.

Her lungs filled with a slow breath of incredible delight as she stared at the shimmering curtain of blue-and-green light swirling about the heavens. It seemed to dance to some silent music.

Not taking her gaze from it for fear it would

disappear, she murmured to Cody, "The northern lights?"

"Yes," Cody confirmed. "Aurora borealis—a symphony of light."

She was awestruck. She remembered looking into a kaleidoscope, as a child amazed by the changing patterns and colors of light; but that had been a poor imitation of the wonders nature could perform. The ever moving curtain seemed to be made of flashing jewels—emerald, jade, sapphire, turquoise—all with the brilliance of diamonds. It whirled about the sky with abandon, writhing and twisting, fading, then blossoming again. It seemed to pulse and throb with a life of its own.

"Are you impressed?" Cody murmured very close to her, and Shannon wondered when he had put his arm around her shoulders. Until that moment she had been too enrapt with the dazzling display to notice. But they were sharing a priceless moment, so no objection surfaced.

"Very," she assured him, and leaned a little closer.

"Some people claim you can actually hear the lights," he said.

Shannon paused to listen. A little tingle ran along her nerve ends when she heard a swishing sound. It was very faint, soft and variating in its rhythm with the dancing lights. Her eyes were rounded when she looked at Cody.

"I can hear them," she insisted in a whisper.

The deepening corners of his mouth teased

her assertion. "That's the wind whispering through the pine needles."

"No, it isn't." She was positive it came from the lights.

"Whatever you're hearing, the scientists claim it doesn't come from the lights," Cody explained without attempting to argue the point.

"What causes the northern lights?" Shannon was enchanted with the dipping, swirling banner of changing color.

"It has something to do with the earth's magnetic field at the North Pole and the solar winds from the sun, which cause a kind of friction." He smiled at her. "It's all very scientific, but theory spoils the illusion of magic."

"Yes," she agreed.

A streak of green light separated itself from the pulsating curtain and seemed to stab at the earth. Shannon gasped at the unexpected change in its dance. Then the entire wave of light appeared to come closer to the ground.

"Maybe it heard us talking," Cody murmured.

"What?" Shannon didn't understand that remark.

"One of the legends of the light is that it will come closer if you talk to it or whistle." He eyed her with a challenging blue gleam. "Why don't you try it?"

Pursing her lips, she whistled softly. There was an almost immediate reaction from the dazzling blue green curtain. It hovered, then seemed to dip earthward.

An eerie thrill ran down Shannon's spine and she tried whistling again. The aurora writhed, seeming to come nearer, then darted away.

"Wrong note, maybe," Cody suggested with an indulgent glance.

"It seemed to respond, though, didn't it?" she said, a little awed.

"But we'll never know if it would have done the same thing if you hadn't whistled," he pointed out.

The iridescent haze began to fade, the brilliant glow becoming dimmer. Shannon held her breath, hoping it would come back, but it was melting and dissolving into the blackness of the night. Tipping her head, she looked at Cody.

"Will it come back?" she whispered.

"I'm afraid the show is over," he replied gently.

The smile on his mouth began to fade as he looked at her. Shannon felt the pulse start to beat loudly in her throat at the disturbing intensity of his gaze. "Another superstition attached to the lights that I failed to mention—" his voice was a husky murmur, spilling over her with caressive force "—is what happens to the people who witness this magical display."

"What happens?" Her own voice had a breathy sound.

"Supposedly...they do things they wouldn't normally do." His darkly blue gaze was touching each feature of her face. His arms were slowly turning her toward him. "It must be more than legend, because I told myself I wouldn't do this again, not until that ring was off your finger."

"Yes." It was a choked little sound, because she felt the inevitability of this moment, too.

When his mouth came down upon hers, she was moving to meet it. Their chemistries mingled with volatile results, producing sensations as fiery and brilliant as any she had witnessed in the sky. His hands tunneled their way inside her bulky jacket, encircling her waist and spreading themselves over her spine and hips to press her to his hard male length.

Desire seared its white heat through her limbs, melting her into the glorious oblivion of his embrace. Her lips parted to discover the fulfillment of his devouring kiss. Nothing else existed in this moment. It belonged only to the two of them.

There was a terrible aching to get closer to him. Shannon strained to satisfy that need. Cody dragged his mouth across her cheek to her neck, roughly nuzzling the vein that pulsed there. His roaming hands were becoming tangled in the loose folds of her flannel nightgown as it defied his attempts to cup the fullness of her breasts in his palms.

"My God, what are you wearing?" he muttered thickly.

A breathless laugh broke from her throat,

brief and disturbed. "My nightgown. It's the granny kind," she murmured.

Cody drank in a deep shuddering breath and rested his forehead against hers. At some point her hands had slipped inside his coat to spread themselves across his chest. She could feel the thundering of his heart.

"Tell me that you still want me to find your fiancé." His voice was heavy and rough in its demand. "Tell me you can still care about him after this. You want me as badly as I want you. Admit it."

The diamond ring on her finger suddenly weighed a ton. She had forgotten and she didn't thank Cody for reminding her. There had been such beauty in the moment—and now it was destroyed by guilt. She breathed in a choked sob of protest.

His grip tightened, his fingers digging into the sides of her waist as if he wanted to shake her. "Admit it," he demanded again. "It's me you want, not him. Your body has already told me. Now I want you to say it."

"Yes." It was a thin sound, an admission even as she pushed away from the temptation of his embrace. She kept her chin lowered, not wanting him to see the anguish and torment in her face.

"You aren't going to marry him," he stated.

"Yes, I am." That's why she had come all this way to Alaska. She loved Rick. There wasn't any way she could be sure she had stopped loving him.

The stillness of Cody was expressive. "You can't mean it!" he flared.

Shannon lifted her head, the aftershocks of his kisses still trembling through her. She was surprised she could act so calm.

"I do mean it," she insisted. "You don't marry a man because of the way he makes your body feel. You marry him because of what's in your heart."

"And you're saying that you still love him?" He was angry; a raging frown creased his expression.

"Yes," Shannon whispered. "As soon as I find him we'll be married." It seemed that she had to say the words to convince herself. Looking at Cody, it was all she could do not to yield to the love she knew she would find in his arms.

He released her with a half-angry shove. "I'll find him for you. I'll find him. But don't invite me to the wedding," he snapped.

With a sharp pivot he stalked off into the night's darkness. She shivered, suddenly very cold. A tear slipped down her cheek and she hurriedly wiped it away. Before she could respond to the impulse to go after him, Shannon hurried toward the cabin.

CHAPTER EIGHT

THE NEXT MORNING Cody barely addressed five
words to her. When he looked at her, which was
seldom, his eyes were blank of expression.
There was no warmth, no laughing glint, no
disturbing light to enthrall her. Shannon had
never felt so forsaken. The loss of even his
friendship left her crushed. She hadn't realized
how important she had allowed him to become
in her life.

There wasn't any way to hide the strain between them. Noah noticed it immediately. All
through breakfast and while they were loading
the plane to take off, his glance kept darting
from one to the other in an effort to catch some
word or phrase that would tell him what had
gone wrong.

Dispirited and confused, Shannon chose to sit
in the rear seat of the aircraft, letting Noah sit
up front in the copilot's seat next to Cody. As he
taxied onto the lake for takeoff, she stared out
the window, blind to the incredible scenery her
eyes beheld.

Once they were airborne, she leaned her head
against the back of her seat and closed her eyes,

covering them with her hand. The steady drone of the engine filled her hearing. She was only half-conscious of Cody communicating with someone on the plane's radio.

Noah's sudden whoop of glee startled her into alertness. Her hand came down as her eyes snapped open. She stared at the older man, who had turned to look at her with a wide grin splitting his face.

"Did you hear that, Shannon?" he asked in unabashed excitement. "Glory be! I thought it was a waste of time!"

"Hear what?" She leaned forward, a bewildered frown on her forehead as she tried to figure out what he was talking about.

"They made it!" he declared.

At that moment Cody put the plane into a steep banking turn, veering onto a new course at a forty-five-degree angle to the one they'd been flying. Shannon's stomach rolled with the pressure of the gravity force before the plane leveled off.

"Who made it? What are you talking about?" she finally responded to Noah's statement.

It was Cody who leaned back to answer, partially turning his head without actually looking at her. "They're alive," he clarified the statement in a bitingly cynical tone. "Rick is alive. They walked out of the mountains. We just got word that they stumbled into a fishing camp this morning."

For a full second the news didn't register. It seemed so impossible to believe, even though she had never doubted for a minute that Rick was alive. It was a case of hearing someone else say the words instead of her.

Relief flooded through her, leaving her suddenly weak. "He's alive," she repeated, although too softly for the men in the front to hear her. She waited for the uplifting tide of joy, but it didn't come. There was just an emptiness—a loss of purpose. She didn't have to look for Rick anymore. He'd been found.

"We're heading for the fishing camp now," Cody stated, raising his hard voice to ensure it was heard above the engine.

"Are they—is he all right?" She finally managed to ask a question.

"The transmission was a little garbled," he told her. "But none of them could be too badly hurt if they were able to walk out of the mountains."

Yes, that was true, Shannon realized, and leaned back in her seat. Any injuries would have had to be minor ones. She caught herself twisting the diamond ring on her finger, trying to ease its constricting band as if it had become too tight. She glanced down at her hand.

"Isn't that wonderful news?" Noah's voice prompted her to look up. "You said all along that he was alive."

"Yes." She forced a smile, then suddenly

found it wasn't so difficult after all. "It's great!"

There was a measure of gladness spilling through her veins. She had expected it to be stronger, but now Shannon was simply relieved to discover it was there at all. She turned her gaze out the window with new interest. Somewhere up ahead Rick was waiting for her. Once she saw him again, everything would be the way it was before. That's what she kept telling herself.

If her glance strayed too often to the man with the pitch-black hair flying the plane—if her heartstrings were tugged by a silent longing— Shannon ignored it. It was a mixture of physical attraction, gratitude for his help and a keen sense of friendship she felt for Cody. It was Rick she loved. It was Rick she was going to marry. Hadn't she said so repeatedly?

Almost two hours later the plane began to descend, aiming for a lake winking in the morning sunlight. An eagerness began to build within Shannon. She made sure her seat belt was fastened tightly long before it was necessary. Automatically she braced herself when the seaplane bumped onto the lake's glistening surface.

Her gaze searched the painted log cabins clustered close to the near shoreline. Other seaplanes were moored near the camp, as well as fishing boats. She scanned the figures of the people but didn't recognize Rick's lanky frame among those walking about the cabin area.

Cody taxied the plane toward the shore. Just before the metal pontoon scraped the graveled bottom of the lake, he cut the engine, which had already been reduced to a slow speed. In a matter of a few minutes Cody was offering her a hand to help her out of the rear seat.

The cool impartiality of his touch chilled her. Her glance briefly met his hard gaze and bounced away. His heady male vigor hadn't dimmed. Its powerful force was simply no longer directed at her. But she continued to be affected by it.

With solid ground beneath her feet, Shannon waited uncertainly for Cody and his father to join her before starting toward the cabins. Noah lagged, fussing with the securing ropes. Shannon sensed the impatience rippling through Cody.

"Come on, dad," he finally summoned the man.

When Noah started forward, Cody turned. His glance fell on Shannon. There was a twist of ironic amusement to his mouth as he silently studied her.

"Why are you looking so hesitant and worried?" he taunted. "This is the big moment, Texas. You should be eager and radiant."

Her chin lifted a notch higher. "I will be," she insisted, "when I see Rick."

"Then let's go," he challenged, and motioned her to lead the way with a mocking gesture of his hand. "We'll probably find him at the office. That seems to be the hub of activity around here.''

Her scanning glance located the cabin with the shingle hanging outside, the word "office" printed on it. She hurried toward the cabin, aware that she was driven more by Cody's urging than by her own.

When she opened the door, there was a hum of voices. The small room was crowded with people, most of them standing and all talking at the same time. Someone made way to let her enter the room.

Shannon wasn't sure whether she saw Rick first or he saw her. All of a sudden he was in front of her—as tall and lanky as she remembered, and with the shock of sandy hair. That was about all the impression she had time to absorb.

"Shannon!" he cried in surprised disbelief.

"Oh, Rick," she gasped his name.

His arms lifted to reach out for her. Some inexorable force impelled her into them. The minute she felt the familiar comfort of his arms, she seemed to relax. Rick was all right. It was suddenly all right to cry.

He must have felt the dampness of her cheek against his skin, because he cupped a hand under her chin and lifted it. "What is this?" Rick chided, and wiped away a tear with a forefinger. "Tears?"

"Yes," she admitted, smiling at him.

Now she could see the cuts and abrasions on

one side of his face, the weariness in his red-rimmed eyes. He seemed to lack that old sparkle of enthusiasm and lust for adventure that she remembered so well. Rick had gone through quite an ordeal and it had left its mark on him. He had matured, Shannon realized. There was a subtle difference to him that she hadn't expected.

"You must have been through hell," he murmured sympathetically. "I kept thinking about you flying in here. I wasn't sure if you'd come—if you had used the ticket I sent you."

"I did. I sent a telegram to let you know when I would arrive, but you never got it. No one seemed to know where you were or where you were working." The whole thing seemed to have happened a long time ago—to some other person.

"I knew you'd be worried half out of your mind," Rick said with a grimace.

"But what about you?" Shannon drew back to look at him. "Are you okay? Were you hurt?"

"I'm fine," Rick assured her. "Some cuts and bruises, a pulled muscle or two, but I'm okay." He didn't seem to want to talk about the crash or its subsequent events. "How did you get here?"

She wasn't able to hold his look, her glance falling away. "Cody brought me."

Shannon half turned to locate him. He and Noah were standing only a few feet away. His light blue eyes seemed to pierce her before they flicked beyond her to Rick.

"Cody Steele." Rick's voice held recognition and vague confusion. It carried to Cody and he stepped forward. Rick turned Shannon to his side and reached out to shake hands with Cody. "Thanks for bringing her here."

"Your fiancée is a very persuasive woman, as well as beautiful," Cody said. "Did she tell you that she's had me out searching for you—or the wreckage of your plane?"

"No, she didn't." Rick glanced at her in surprise. "I wrote you about him, didn't I?"

"Yes," she nodded.

"He's the best damned bush pilot there is," Rick declared, not at all hesitant about voicing his admiration.

"That's for sure." Noah was quick to agree with Rick's assessment.

A serious look stole across Rick's face. "I wish you had been along—although I don't know if it would have changed anything."

"You were lucky," Cody stated.

"Yeah." Rick nodded with smiling emphasis, then attempted to joke. "As the old saying goes, it's a good landing if you can walk away from it." He shrugged a shoulder. "In this case we crawled, but I guess it still qualifies under the heading of a good landing."

"What happened?" Cody asked.

"There was a storm." Rick shook his head as if he weren't too clear about the events. "Before we knew it we were lost. Then we lost power. There was a leak in the oil line, we discovered afterward. I don't see how Henderson kept it in the air as long as he did.''

"He's a regular Houdini," Noah declared.

"Let's go over there, Shannon, so I can introduce you to him," Rick suggested, directing her toward another circle of people. "I want you to meet Mr. Hale...and his daughter, too," he added, faltering a little.

The pilot was a burly man with silver hair. Rick made the introductions, but Shannon wasn't allowed to do more than acknowledge them. Henderson was being attended by a physician who had been flown in to examine the survivors of the plane crash and supply whatever medical aid they needed. Henderson had suffered a dislocated shoulder in the crash and had some nasty cuts on the forehead that needed stitches.

Then Rick guided her to the father-daughter pair. Jackson Hale did not remind Shannon of an oil company executive. He looked like an outdoorsman, a beard growth covering his cheeks and jaw.

He observed the notice Shannon gave it and rubbed the grizzled whiskers on his chin. "It's new," he explained. "I don't want to forget what a narrow escape I had, so I've decided not to shave it off." Then he glanced at Rick. "Is she the fiancée you were always talking about?"

"Yes," Rick admitted, and Shannon realized

that he had simply introduced her by name without explaining her relationship to him.

"That's quite a young man you have there, young lady," Jackson Hale stated. "I hope you know that."

"I do." She smiled and happened to look up—straight into Cody's eyes. The blue of his eyes was polar; their lightness had crystals of ice in them.

Jackson Hale was talking again, and Shannon tore her gaze from Cody. "Rick kept me going when I was ready to quit. He was determined we were going to get out of those mountains. Looking at you, I can see why," he smiled.

"Thank you," she murmured in response to his compliment.

Noah inserted himself into the conversation. "I guess they're two of a kind. Shannon kept insisting her fiancé was alive even when everybody else had given you all up for dead. She twisted Cody's arm until he agreed to come looking for you."

"I'm going to be upset if I don't get an invitation to your wedding," Jackson Hale warned Rick. "She was flying up here to marry you, wasn't she?"

"Yes." Rick nodded stiffly, an uneven smile on his mouth. "Of course, there have been a few delays along the way."

"And a few more to come, I imagine," Shannon said, since it was obvious that after all Rick had been through, they wouldn't rush right out and get married.

"Where are you staying?" the oil company chairman inquired.

"At the Westward," she replied.

"Why didn't you stay at my apartment?" Rick frowned. "It would have been perfectly all right. I mean, your folks couldn't have objected, since I wasn't there at the time."

"I hate to tell you this, but your apartment has been rented to new tenants," she informed him with a gentle smile. "It seems your rent was due, and when you didn't show up, the manager packed your things and let it out to someone else."

"He what?" Then Rick sighed. "I guess he didn't know, either."

"No. I stored your things at the hotel with mine," Shannon added.

"Rick, have you introduced your fiancée to my daughter?" Jackson Hale asked, as if just realizing himself that the silent figure sitting on the floor beside his chair hadn't joined in the conversation.

"I'm not sure if I did," Rick murmured uncertainly.

The young woman had been so unobtrusive that Shannon had barely noticed her at all. She studied her now, noting the triangular rips in the expensive blouse and the red scratches on an otherwise flawless complexion. The blonde's hair was disheveled, a bramble caught in one curl. The evidence of physical exhaustion was in her posture, her body loose and tired.

"Belinda, I'd like you to meet Rick's fiancée, Miss Shannon Hayes," her father introduced them, correcting the unintentional slight.

"How do you do, Miss Hayes?" The blond girl's voice was very cultured, but the hand she extended was chapped and rough.

"It's my pleasure," Shannon returned, and leaned down to shake her hand so the weary girl wouldn't have to rise.

"Let me get you a chair to sit on, Belinda," Rick volunteered, and started to move away.

"Don't bother, Rick," she called him back, smiling stiffly. "I've got used to sitting on hard things—whether it's the ground or the floor."

"Yes," her father laughed. "This is one princess who has learned to sleep on the pea."

Outside there was the whirring noise of a helicopter. It drowned out all the conversation in the room, bringing it to a standstill. Dust kicked up by the whirling blades billowed outside the windows as the helicopter landed at the camp. When the noise died to just the chop-chop of the blades, Jackson Hale smiled.

"The company said they were sending a jet copter to pick us up," he said. "I guess that's it." He laid an affectionate hand on his daughter's shoulder. "We'll be leaving for Anchorage in another twenty minutes. How does that sound?"

"Wonderful." There was little feeling in her

voice, but Shannon guessed that Belinda was too tired to be very enthusiastic.

"You'll fly back with us, won't you, Miss Hayes?" Jackson inquired.

"I don't know." She glanced uncertainly at Cody.

His mouth slanted in a twisting smile. "You surely aren't thinking of separating from your fiancé when you just reunited with him?"

His remark aroused her stubborn streak. She turned back to the whiskered man. "If you think there's room—" she began.

"Of course there's room," he interrupted. "If there isn't, we'll leave somebody else behind."

Cody moved, crossing the short distance between them at a leisurely pace. Yet the air seemed to crackle with sexual tension when he stopped beside her. Shannon held her breath, sensing the irritated impatience that seemed to churn inside him.

"Since you're flying back with them, dad and I will shove off," he stated, his light eyes watching her every flicker of movement.

"Yeah," Noah inserted. "I'll see that your bag gets put on the chopper."

"I really must thank you again for helping Shannon," Rick said, standing at her side, yet not touching her or claiming her with a possessive arm.

"Don't worry, Rick." Cody smiled crookedly. "Thanks aren't needed. As it turns out, I did it for nothing." She didn't have an opportunity to move or offer resistance as his hands closed on her upper arms, holding her still. "Goodbye, Texas."

His mouth covered hers while she was still trying to guess his intentions. His kiss was rawly hungry, devouring her lips and eroding her carefully erected defenses. All too quickly he was holding her at arm's length. Then he brought her partway back, bending his head to murmur in her ear.

"You marry him, Shannon," he said huskily. "And forget me—if you can."

Tears stung her eyes as Shannon glared at him. It was a cruel parting, heavily tinged with bitterness. Cody slanted a challenging look at Rick, then walked out.

"You take care of her," Noah admonished Rick, then shuffled hurriedly after his son.

Rick studied her with a curious frown. "What was that all about?" he murmured.

At the moment her pride needed protecting as much as anything. So she tried not to let it show that Cody's bitter words had hurt. "Like Cody said," she said airily, "it was nothing."

CHAPTER NINE

NIGHT WAS FALLING GENTLY outside the windows of Shannon's hotel in Anchorage. Rick had taken a room there, as well, but at the moment he was in hers, stretched out on the couch with his head resting on her lap. They had dined together earlier at the restaurant on the top floor where Cody had met her that first night in Alaska.

Shannon had talked to Rick about him—but not about the intimate moments or the way she had responded so ardently to his kisses. She had made her relationship with Cody sound light-hearted and full of fun, relating the way he had teased her about Texas and how staunchly Noah had looked after her reputation. They had both laughed over it, although there had been a faintly hollow ring to hers.

Somehow they had talked all around the real issue—each other and their future plans. Even when they had telephoned her parents after dinner, they had both avoided giving a specific date for their postponed wedding.

"Did I tell you?" Rick looked up at her while her fingers absently curled in his sandy hair.

"Mr. Hale says I have a job flying for his company for as long as I want."

"That's wonderful," Shannon smiled.

"When I crawled out of the wreckage of that plane," Rick sighed, "I really thought I'd blown my chances of ever working in Alaska. There it was, my first flying job, and we crash with the top man of the company on board. Now it sounds funny, but at the time...." His head moved to the side in a show of hopelessness.

"I can guess," she murmured, but inwardly she was thinking that if she were on a couch with Cody they probably wouldn't be talking. "What was it like—finding your way out, I mean?"

"Frustrating." There was a lot of feeling in that one word. "Every time we went around another bend—we saw another mountain. There wasn't a sign of another living soul."

"The pilot must have been in a lot of pain with that dislocated shoulder," Shannon remembered.

"Henderson never complained." Rick paused and stared at the ceiling, seeming to look beyond it. "I wasn't too impressed with Belinda when I first met her on the flight. I thought she was 'daddy's spoiled darling.'" A faint smile curved his mouth. "But I wish you could have seen her. After she stopped fussing about her hair and the bugs and the food, she turned out to be a real trouper."

Belinda again, Shannon thought. It seemed that every time Rick turned around he was mentioning her name. Was she being overly sensitive to his interest in another woman? She didn't think so. There was no resentment— nothing that resembled jealousy. Maybe it was just a simple observation.

"She seemed nice." Actually, Shannon hadn't formed any real impression of the blonde. There hadn't been an opportunity to talk to her on the flight to Anchorage. The noise of the helicopter precluded any conversation except with the person sitting next to her—which had been Rick.

"She's terrific." Rick was more positive in his reply. Then he had to smother a yawn with his hand. "Sorry—" he smiled in apology at her "—that wasn't any reflection on present company." He pushed himself into a sitting position. "I'm really bushed, Shannon. Do you mind if we have an early night?"

"Of course not," she assured him.

As she stood up to walk him to the door, he took her hand. "You are one terrific gal, too." He kissed her lightly. "I meant to tell you that before."

"You are one terrific guy," she countered. "And I meant to tell you that before."

When he kissed her again, this time Rick took her in his arms. There was nothing demanding about the embrace. It was warm and comfortable. But she definitely saw no northern lights display. She told herself she didn't mind.

Slowly drawing back, Rick studied her with a peculiar intensity, as if seeing her for the first time. Shannon was a little confused.

"Good night," he murmured. "I'll call you in the morning."

"Sleep late," she urged. "The rest will do you good."

"Okay." Rick didn't need persuading.

There was one more light kiss—a peck, really—then Rick was leaving her to walk to the door. Shannon watched him go, waving a hand when he looked back before entering the hotel corridor and closing the door.

Whether she liked the idea or not, she was mentally comparing Rick and Cody. The scales were starting to tip heavily in Cody's favor. Seeing Rick again and being with him had started to unmask some of the feelings she had tried to hide.

It was entirely possible that she didn't love Rick. She cared about him very much, but it wasn't the same. Shannon was slowly realizing that. Her teeth sank into her lower lip as she remembered she had told Cody that you married someone because of what you felt in your heart, not your body. Yet Cody affected her in both places.

She was suddenly stabbed by the thought that she might never see him again. She did love him. How could she have been so blind all this time? Because of Rick? Because of her loyalty—her promise to him? Shannon couldn't even begin to guess.

But to marry Rick would be the worst mistake she'd ever make in her life. You don't marry one man when you're in love with another—as she was.

There was a light tap on the door. At first Shannon thought it was someone knocking at another door. Then the sound came again. A slight frown clouded her expression as she crossed the room to the door. It was probably Rick. Hope swelled that it might be Cody.

Both guesses were wrong. When she opened the door, Belinda Hale was standing in the hallway—a very different version from the tattered and weary blonde Shannon had met at the fishing camp. She practically oozed sophistication in her designer suit, wearing imported perfume and with her hair professionally coiffed.

"If you're looking for Rick," Shannon guessed, "he just left a few minutes ago. He was going to his room."

"I know." It was a calm answer. "I waited in the fire stairs until he left because I wanted to talk to you. May I come in?" Belinda asked with absolute politeness.

A little stunned, Shannon stepped back to admit her. "Yes. Please come in." There was a little flourish of formalities as each made sure the other was comfortably seated. "You said you wanted to speak to me?" Shannon prompted, her curiosity aroused and her intuition already working.

"Yes," Belinda confirmed the fact again, primly crossing her legs. "You've probably already guessed why I'm here."

"I'm not sure, no." Shannon wasn't about to speculate. It might be too embarrassing if she were wrong.

"I'm in love with Rick." Belinda came straight to the point, not challenging or blunt in her tone, but speaking very calmly. "I'm sure you'll say—as my father has said—that the attachment I feel to Rick springs from the circumstances that threw us together. I'll admit that the crash sped up the process, but I love him just the same."

"Does...does he know this?" Shannon wondered.

"I told him, but he seemed to think I didn't know what I was saying, either." Belinda smiled. There was an indulgent quality in her tone, as if Rick needed to be humored, which he often did. "What else could he say? He's engaged to you. My father's money and position don't help—not with Rick."

"Why are you telling me all this?" Shannon was a little amazed by the woman's audacity, although she admired it, too.

The announcement didn't upset her—obviously not, when she'd already made up her mind that it was Cody she loved instead of Rick. She had every intention of returning the engagement ring to Rick in the morning. But she kept silent about all that because her interest was piqued by this forthright and very stunning blond girl.

"You didn't know me before the plane crash, Miss Hayes, but I have done a lot of growing up in a very short time." Her initial explanation only confused Shannon further. "Once I thought I knew how to handle every adult situation. I was *extremely* adult. I was engaged to a man who possessed all the qualities I wanted in a husband. Unfortunately, he was still in love with his ex-wife. At the time I smiled and insisted it was better that we discovered that before we were married. I went blithely on my way—and they were remarried."

"I see," Shannon murmured when Belinda paused, but she didn't really see at all.

"It was only after I met Rick that I discovered I hadn't been in love with...my previous fiancé. I didn't even know what life was all about," she stated.

"And now you do." It seemed the logical conclusion to that remark, Shannon thought.

"I think you have a fair idea of my background—the type of family and home life I've known," Belinda went on. "So I'm sure you won't be surprised to hear me say that virtually everything I've ever wanted has been handed to me. I've never had to struggle for anything... until the plane crash. That's when I learned how to fight for what I wanted."

"And you are here because you're in love with Rick." She began to realize where the entire conversation had been leading.

"Yes. He's engaged to you, so by all rights I should keep my hands off him. Once I would have—even if I loved him. But not anymore." Belinda paused slightly. "I came tonight to give you fair warning that I intend to fight to take Rick away from you."

"I don't think it will be much of a fight." Shannon was going to explain her own personal decision.

"He doesn't love you. He hasn't accepted that yet, but he doesn't love you," she insisted.

"It will make it easier if he doesn't, because I don't love him."

She finally had the socialite's attention. "But you're engaged to him," Belinda frowned.

"Not for long," Shannon replied. "I have decided to give him back the ring. Things have changed. I've changed. So has Rick. I noticed it tonight."

"Are you sure?" The very calm, very controlled girl was suddenly flustered. "You aren't just saying that?"

"If I had any hesitation before, it was a desire not to hurt Rick," Shannon explained. "I care about him a lot, and I want him to be happy, but I don't love him."

A soft sigh came from Belinda. Shannon watched her relax, only now seeing how tense she had been—a coiled spring inside despite the smooth facade.

"I don't know what to say," Belinda murmured—and Shannon guessed it was a new experience.

"I do," she smiled. "Good luck. And I hope you invite me to the wedding."

"I will," Belinda promised, her eyes sparkling with tears as she stood up. "You can bet on it." She hesitated. "Will you tell Rick that I came to see you?"

Shannon thought about it a minute, then nodded. "Yes, I believe I will. It might be just what it takes to convince him."

"Thank you." She looked radiant and even more beautiful—if that were possible. "You are very nice, Shannon." She used her given name for the first time. "I can see why Rick wanted to marry you."

"Being nice isn't the same as being in love," she replied. "And that's something I just learned, too."

After Belinda had left the room, Shannon felt immeasurably better about her decision to break the engagement. Even if things didn't work out between Rick and Belinda, it was still the right thing to do.

And there was Cody. As soon as she gave the ring back, she'd call him. That prospect brought a beaming smile to her face.

IT WAS LATE THE NEXT MORNING when Rick called to suggest they have breakfast together—or lunch if Shannon had already eaten. She let her acceptance of the invitation be implied and asked him to come by her room.

Breaking their engagement was a personal thing, and she didn't want to do it in a public restaurant or over the telephone. After Shannon had ended her brief conversation with him, she called room service to send up some coffee. It and Rick arrived at the same time.

"What is this?" he asked with a questioning glance. "I thought we were going down to the coffee shop."

"I wanted to talk to you first," she explained, and poured them each a cup. "You look rested this morning," Shannon observed as she handed him a cup of coffee.

The weariness was gone from his face and that zestiness was back. Even that eager thirst for adventure had returned. His tall lanky frame seemed to be bursting with energy. Shannon could see a lot of the old Rick in him, but the subtle changes were still there.

"I slept like a log," he admitted, and folded his slim, long-boned body onto the couch. He took a sip of the coffee. "Ahh, that hits the spot," he declared, and sent a questioning glance at her. "What did you want to talk to me about?"

"I had a visitor last night after you left," Shannon began.

"Who?" Rick lifted a curious brow. "Cody?"

His guess startled her. "No," she quickly

denied that. "What made you think he would come?"

"From what you said last night—" Rick studied the coffee in his cup rather than look at her "—I gathered he was interested in you. He is, isn't he?"

"Yes. Or at least he acts as if he is." Last night she had realized that Cody had never said he loved her. Of course, he might not have wanted to while Rick's ring was on her finger. "With Cody it's hard to tell when to take him seriously."

"I suppose so." His answer wasn't really an agreement. "Who was here last night, then?"

"Belinda Hale," Shannon answered.

Rick's head jerked up. A hint of guilt swept across his expression before he covered it with grimness. "Why did she come to see you?"

"She is in love with you, Rick," Shannon said, tipping her head slightly to one side. "But you know that, don't you?"

"I know what she's told me." He was upset and trying to contain it. "I probably should have explained what happened out there. You have a right to know. I kissed her a few times and. . . ." Rick paused, grimly reddening.

"You don't need to explain," Shannon interrupted.

"I do," Rick insisted. "There were times when it seemed we were Adam and Eve out there. I know that isn't an excuse, but—"

"It's a better excuse than I had when Cody

kissed me," she reminded him, and watched him hesitate. "A lot has happened to both of us since you gave me this ring. We've changed. I don't think either of us feels the same. Am I right?"

"I. . . ." He didn't finish the sentence as he looked at her with deep regret. "The last thing I want to do is hurt you, Shannon. You've come all this way to Alaska to marry me."

But he didn't love her. Even though he hadn't said it, she knew it. She twisted the ring off her finger and handed it to him, smiling gently.

"But I don't love you the way I should, Rick," she declared when he hesitated at taking the ring. "And it has nothing to do with you and Belinda. If you want to blame someone, Cody is the most likely candidate. He made me see that if I really loved you, I wouldn't have been attracted to him."

"Are you sure?" Rick didn't want any doubts.

"Yes. I'd already made up my mind to give this back to you last night before Belinda came," she admitted. "But I was concerned about the way you would take it. The things she told me just made the decision an easier one."

Finally he took the ring from her and studied the play of rainbow light on the square-cut diamond. With a shake of his head, Rick looked at her, affection warming his eyes.

"Shannon, I don't know what to say," he murmured.

"Belinda said the same thing last night," she remembered with a dimpling smile. "She loves you. Why don't you call her?"

"It would never work." He ran a hand through his straw-colored hair. "I'm nothing but a flight jockey. She's the boss's daughter."

"You said she was quite a trouper; don't forget that," Shannon advised. "Finish your coffee and call her. She's probably waiting to hear from you."

Rick did just that.

CHAPTER TEN

THE CAB PULLED UP in front of the hangar at Merrill Field and stopped. There was light in Shannon's eyes as she read the sign Steele Air atop the attached concrete-block building that served as an office.

For three days she had been trying to talk to Cody, but he was always out—off somewhere on a charter. She'd left messages for him to phone her, but he hadn't called. Twice she had almost told Noah about her broken engagement, but she wanted to make the announcement to Cody herself. She was determined to see him, which was why she had come to the charter service. She was prepared to haunt the place if necessary.

Paying the cabby, she stepped out of the taxi and walked toward the door. The sun was shining on the Chugach Mountains surrounding Anchorage. A few powder-puff clouds were in the sky and the air was brisk with autumn.

Although nervous, she was comforted by memories of the first time she'd gone there. She even paused to wipe her high-heeled boots on the bristled mat outside the door, just as she had done the last time.

Inside it was just the way she remembered it: magazines scattered around, the coffee table littered with used Styrofoam cups, and a couple of weary pilots sprawled on the couch. Except this time the swivel chair behind the desk wasn't empty. Noah was sitting in it. He pushed to his feet when he saw her. Her sweeping glance noted that the door to Cody's office was closed.

"Well, if you aren't a sight for sore eyes!" Noah declared, and came around the desk to greet her.

"Hello, Noah. It's good to see you again." She smiled warmly.

"What are you doin' here?" he asked in his familiar raspy voice. "I figured you'd be busy with your wedding plans and findin' yourselves a place to live."

"I came to see Cody. Is he in?" She glanced toward the door, then noticed Noah shift uncomfortably.

"He's in," he admitted. "But he ain't been himself lately. He's been snapping at just about everybody—including me," he added with a wounded look. "I don't think it would be a good idea if you saw him just now. He just got back from a long flight and he's kinda tired and extra cranky."

"I'll take my chances." Nothing was going to stop her from seeing him. It was there in the determined lift of her chin.

Noah shook his head, doubting the wisdom of her decision. "I'll tell him you're here," he said, and moved in his shuffling gait toward the closed door. "But the mood he's in, he just might throw you out. I keep tellin' him it's bad for business, but he won't listen to me."

Shannon followed and paused behind him when Noah knocked twice on the door. Cody's voice was muffled, but the door didn't shut out its harshness.

"What is it?" he demanded from the private office.

Noah sent her a grimacing look, then turned the doorknob, opening the door a crack. "You've got a visitor, Cody." All she could see was a corner of the desk in the room.

"Who is it?" Impatience and ill temper stirred the question.

Before Noah could answer, Shannon laid a hand on his arm, then shouldered her way past him and pushed the door the rest of the way open to enter the room. Cody was seated behind the desk, his sun-bronzed features set in uncompromising lines. His expression didn't change when he saw her, but she felt his light eyes rake over her figure and saw the narrowing of his mouth.

"What do you want?" Cody looked away, not bothering to rise to greet her when she walked in. He focused all his attention on the report he was writing.

"I've been trying to reach you." She heard the click of the latch as Noah closed the door behind her. "You never returned any of my calls."

"I've been busy," he countered, without looking up from his papers. "I have a company to run. The work piled up while I was gone."

He certainly wasn't making it easy for her. "I never did have a chance to thank you for all you did for me." Shannon realized how much of his valuable time she had used.

His dark head lifted, the light blue of his eyes centering on her. "So now you've thanked me," Cody stated. "If there's nothing else, I have work to do. I can't spare any time for idle chit-chat."

A little thread of anger ran through her nerves. "I came to tell you that Rick and I—" But he didn't give her a chance to complete the sentence.

He pushed out of the chair with a suppressed violence. "I told you I didn't want an invitation to your wedding. I don't even want to know when it is!" Cody snapped, a cold rage darkening his features.

"There isn't going to be a wedding!" Shannon flashed. "That's what I came to tell you." She showed him her left hand, bare of any engagement ring.

Cody made no move toward her, his gaze inspecting her hand, then lifting to her face. "When did this happen?"

"Three days ago," she answered, and waited for some sign to show it mattered to him—a hint of pleasure or satisfaction. "You were right. I didn't love him."

"It damn well took you long enough to find it out," he grumbled in irritation.

He didn't seem pleased at all. Shannon gathered up her pride, standing stiffly. "That's what I came to tell you. And to say thanks for your help."

"What will you do now?" Cody shot the question at her. "I suppose you're flying back to Texas now that the engagement is off."

"Yes." She hadn't made any plans yet. She'd hoped.... "I thought I'd make reservations to leave this weekend." Her fingers tightened on her shoulder bag. "So I guess this is goodbye, as well." She turned to walk to the door, tears burning her eyes.

"Like hell it is!" Long strides carried him around the desk after her; he caught her before she reached the door, his arms turning her around. "You aren't going anywhere, Texas!"

After the cold shoulder he'd given her, Shannon wasn't about to melt into his arms even if that was what she wanted to do. "Why should I stay here?" she challenged.

That lazy light came back to his bold eyes. "Because you love me." His hand cupped her cheek, his fingers tunneling into her hair. The warmth of his touch spread across her skin. "That's really why you came here today, isn't it?"

"I never said that." She tried to resist the desire to respond, to remain passive under his spell, but awareness of him was shooting through her.

"No," Cody agreed. "You've denied it every time I've tried to convince you that it's true. You had to put us both through all this useless agony."

When he lowered his head toward her, Shannon instinctively lifted hers to meet his descending mouth halfway. His kiss staked its possession of her as his arm circled her waist to draw her against his body. Her hands slid around his strong shoulders and into the virile thickness of his hair. Happiness flamed inside her, burning away the last remnants of resistance.

Her shoulder purse got in the way, and Cody slipped it off her bringing her arm momentarily down to her side before she returned it to his neck. He gave the purse a little toss so that it landed with a thump on the floor nearby. Then his arms were molding her to his hard length, shaping her soft curves to his masculine contours.

His passion deepened and burned, showing her one of the many sides of love. She reeled under the glorious force of it, wanting to love him completely and forever.

Neither of them heard the door open. They weren't aware of any intrusion until his father issued an astonished, "Cody! What are you doing?" There was a rasp of reproval in the demand as Noah quickly shut the door so no one in the outer office could see the embracing couple.

Cody's arms tightened, not allowing even a discreet distance to come between them when he lifted his head, a disturbing half smile touching his mouth as he looked at her. Shannon was dazzled by the light blazing in his eyes.

"I'm kissing the bride, dad," he replied, and the breath she'd taken became caught in her throat at his answer.

"Well, you shouldn't be doing it like that," his father admonished. "A person could get the wrong idea. Why, if her fiancé had seen that, I wouldn't blame him if he punched you out."

"You're looking at her fiancé, dad," Cody stated, and his smile deepened at the radiance that swept across her face.

"I don't remember 'your asking me," Shannon murmured.

"A small oversight," he insisted with a mocking look. "If you want to be technical, I don't remember that you accepted."

"Would somebody mind telling me what's going on here?" Noah demanded in exasperation. "How can she marry you when she's engaged to someone else?"

Considering the role Noah had played, Shannon thought it only fair to explain the situation to her future father-in-law. "I'm not engaged to Rick anymore." She showed him her bare ring finger. "I gave the ring back to him."

"Now mine will go there," Cody stated. "You can't keep us apart anymore, dad."

"Well, if this don't beat all!" Noah exclaimed, and came forward, extending a gnarled hand to Shannon. "Congratulations. I didn't think this boy of mine would ever settle down with a gal. I hoped it would be someone like you."

Cody was forced to relax his hold on her so she could accept his father's congratulations. "You have been wonderful to me, Noah. I haven't thanked you for that."

"You can thank me by giving me some grandkids," he replied with a knowing wink. "How big a family are you planning? I'd sure like to have a granddaughter and a grandson."

"Dad, would you mind if I married the girl before you started planning our family?" Cody requested with tolerant affection.

"When are you going to marry her? When's the wedding?" he asked. "I'm gonna have to buy me a new suit for the occasion."

"We'll be married just as soon as Shannon's parents can fly up here," Cody stated, then glanced at Shannon and added, almost as an afterthought, "All right?"

"Yes," she assured him, love shining from her eyes.

With an effort Cody dragged his glance from her face. "Dad, will you get out of here? I'd like to be alone with my future wife, if you don't mind."

"Well, just see to it that you behave yourself." Noah reluctantly agreed to leave, but not without advising his son not to take advantage of the situation.

"Go," Cody ordered with dry amusement.

"I'm going, I'm going," Noah muttered, and shuffled to the door.

When they were alone again, Cody gathered her back into his arms, nuzzling her cheek and the hollow of her ear. She felt him shudder.

"I don't know if you have any idea what I've been through these past few days," he murmured thickly. "I thought you were really going to marry him. Why did it take you so long to realize you didn't love him? Do you realize the time we've wasted?"

"Yes," she admitted. "But I guess I had to see Rick again to know that I didn't love him— not the way I thought I did. He's nice and I like him, but it's you I want to marry."

"I've been waiting to hear that since the first time you walked in that door," Cody declared.

She drew back to study his face. "You knew that long ago?" she frowned. "How?"

"I don't know *how* I knew." His fingers traced the curve of her cheek and paused near her lips, underlining their softness. "But the minute you walked through that door, I knew you were the girl I'd been waiting for. It was a rude discovery to find out you were wearing another man's ring on your finger. It complicated the situation considerably."

"So did your father," Shannon smiled.

"Yes." Laughter danced in his eyes and he

chuckled. "My dad is one of a kind. He's bound to do more than his share of interfering."

"I like him." She knew Noah's interference was always motivated by the best of intentions.

Cody kissed her hard. "I always knew that Alaska and Texas would make an unbeatable combination," he declared, and covered her lips again to prove it.